P9-DMA-912

THE ANGEL OF
BASTOGNE

© 2005 by Gilbert Morris
All rights reserved
Printed in the United States of America

13-digit ISBN: 978-0-8054-3291-6
10-digit ISBN: 0-8054-3291-4

Published by Broadman & Holman Publishers,
Nashville, Tennessee

Dewey Decimal Classification: F
Subject Headings: CHRISTMAS—FICTION
                    WORLD WAR, 1939–1945—FICTION

1 2 3 4 5 6 7 8 9 10 09 08 07 06 05

THE **ANGEL** OF
BASTOGNE

a Novel

GILBERT MORRIS

BROADMAN
&HOLMAN
PUBLISHERS

NASHVILLE, TENNESSEE

I dedicate this book to
three of my family who mean a lot to me.

To Doug Freeman—who fought for us all in the Real War.
To Jimmy Jordan—a sweet guy and my friend
since we were rug rats.
To Gale Towne—my fellow pilgrim
on the way to the Celestial City.

Chapter ONE

A freezing blast of air struck the scrawny ginger-colored squirrel just as he emerged from the hole in the top of the large spruce tree. The cold wind caused the little animal to close his eyes, but a fierce hunger drove him out of his warm lair into the frigid air. He scrambled out of the hole, clung to a limb that extended laterally, and for a moment searched the surrounding areas. Something had happened to his world, but he did not know what it was, and fear had kept him inside his nest for days. He did not understand the tremendous blasts that sometimes shook his tree, and now that he was out everything seemed changed. Many trees were down, others were stripped of their foliage, and the forest that had been his lifetime home was gone.

Hunger gnawing at his belly, he scrambled down the tree and began searching frantically for something to fill it. Finally he found an acorn, somewhat moldy, but still food. Grasping it firmly in his tiny paws, he hoisted himself into a sitting position, his tail twitching feverishly.

The squirrel had almost finished the acorn when suddenly that inner sense animals have set off an alarm. He froze, aware that an enemy was near, swiveled his head about, and then for an instant stood as still as any stone statue. Not twenty feet away from him a creature was watching, and he was so frightened that he could not move. He sat there with his paws together, looking a little like a monk at prayer.

Sergeant William Raines had the tiny squirrel exactly in the sight of his M1. All he had to do was pull the trigger, and the creature would be blasted into bits. Willie hesitated, thinking of the first squirrel he'd ever killed. It had been on his tenth birthday at his grandfather's farm in Ohio. The two of them had gone out into the tall pine woods, and Willie had managed to kill three squirrels with his single-shot twenty-two. His grandfather had killed several with his ten-gauge shotgun, and the two of them had come back with their coarse feed sacks filled. As Willie held the bead on the squirrel that stared at him with bright, fear-filled eyes, he remembered how they had skinned the squirrels, dressed them, and then taken them in for his grandmother to cook.

From far away came the rapid stutter of machine-gun fire, but Willie was so accustomed to this he did not move his eyes from the prey in front of him. He was thinking of how delicious the squirrel stew was and how his grandfather had taught him that the best part of a squirrel was the brains mixed up with scrambled eggs.

The memory did something to Willie, and suddenly he laughed and lowered the M1. "Merry Christmas, Mister Squirrel." He grinned as the squirrel raced frantically across the ground, flew up the tree, and popped back into his hole.

Willie brought the rifle back over the lip of the foxhole and sat down, leaning his helmet back against the edge. "You wouldn't have made a mouthful anyway. It would take ten like you to make a good stew."

A German shell shrieked like a wild thing overhead, and Willie ducked his head and closed his eyes. He gripped the rifle until his fingers were white. Finally the explosion came, rocking the earth, but it was not in Willie's foxhole, so he expelled his breath and opened his eyes. Pulling his helmet off, he rubbed his reddish hair, then jammed the helmet back on.

The temperature had dropped far below freezing, making simple existence a struggle. The wind made a constant moan as it drove the tiny flakes of snow across the crust that covered the ground.

Willie desperately wanted to sleep but knew he must not. After seventy-two days of savage fighting in Holland in Operation Market Garden, he and his buddies in the 101st and 82nd Airborne had expected to be sent back to England for R and R.

Instead, they had been crowded into trucks and rushed to meet the might of the German Wehrmacht. Hitler had decided to hit the American army that was driving toward Berlin with everything the German army had left. General McAuliffe was given a simple order: "Hold Bastogne." The Germans threw everything they had at the American force: tanks, Stuka dive-bombers, artillery, and waves of crack SS infantry.

The American forces had no winter clothing, little food, almost no medical supplies, and worst of all, little ammo to face the onslaught. The Germans had surrounded Bastogne, and there was no relief in sight for the 101st and the 82nd.

As Willie Raines sat in his foxhole, his eyes shut against the bitter wind, he wished desperately that he were back home. He tried to think of where he would rather be: at a Cubs baseball game in the hot sun, eating a hot dog and drinking a big Coke. All of that seemed a million miles away, farther than the stars that winked faintly at night over the landscape.

A crunching sound brought Willie upright. Quickly he grasped his rifle, thrust it over the edge of the foxhole, and blinked against the icy particles that bit into his eyes. He kept his M1 off safety and raised it to his shoulder, following a vague movement coming out of the woods to his right. He saw two soldiers and watched as they took a detour around a huge fallen tree that had been uprooted by heavy artillery fire two days ago. Recognizing them, he expelled his breath and called out, "Hey, you two, what are you—"

But his words were cut off when a shell exploded twenty yards from where the two soldiers were located. Both men made a mad dash. Willie had no chance to do more than holler, "Hey?!" when Billy Bob Watkins and Charlie Delaughter landed on him. He was crushed to the bottom of the foxhole, lost his grip on his rifle, and one of the soldiers' feet caught him on the neck and the side of his head. If he hadn't had a helmet on, his head would have been crushed.

"Get off of me, you idiots!"

Billy Bob Watkins, a gangling eighteen-year-old from Bald Knob, Arkansas, rearranged himself, folding his lanky body into the foxhole. His face was lined with fatigue, and his mouth was a straight line. Ordinarily he was a cheerful young man, but the incessant attacks of the German Wehrmacht had drained him as it had the rest of the 101st Airborne who had come to hold the line at Bastogne. Shoving his helmet back, he grinned tightly. "You got anything to eat, Sarge?"

"No!"

"Shucks! I'd shore know what to do with some collards and grits." He slumped down and heaved a weary sigh. "I'm so tard you could scrape it off with a stick."

"What have you got to be tired about? All you've done is fight off the whole German army." Charlie Delaughter shoved Billy Bob away, making room for himself in the fox-hole. His Boston accent contrasted violently with Billy Bob's southern drawl. Carefully he lifted his head over the edge of the foxhole, then drew it back quickly as a shot punctuated the cold air. A tiny branch cut by the passing bullet fluttered down landing on Charlie's head.

Billy Bob reached over and plucked the small branch from Delaughter's helmet. "Them Krauts is a mite touchy, ain't they, now?"

"I thought the fight was out of them, but it's not," Charlie observed.

"Why, them Krauts is just mean, is what they are," Billy Bob nodded sagely, "mean as a junkyard dog. They're born that way."

Delaughter winked at Willie. "I thought you rebels could whip anybody. All you've done is brag about how we'd already be in Berlin if we were tough as the Confederate army."

"Why, shoot, Charlie, if we had some *real* soldiers like them boys who fought under Marse Robert—and some *real* generals like Stonewall Jackson—we'd have nailed that ol' Hitler's hide to the smokehouse wall long 'fore now!"

Willie listened with half his mind to the argument between Billy Bob and Charlie over the Civil War. Each of them had family who'd fought in that earlier war (on opposite sides, of course!), but strangely enough the two had become fast friends. They were almost exactly the same age, but Delaughter, who was only three days older, drove Billy Bob to distraction by referring to himself as "the old man," and to Billy Bob as "Junior."

Charlie Delaughter asked suddenly, "What's the date, Sarge?"

"What difference does it make?" Willie demanded, staring at him. "You got an appointment at the dentist?"

"It's December the twenty-fifth, 1944," Billy Bob grinned. He reached over and punched Willie on the arm hard. "Merry Christmas. What time do we eat the turkey, Sarge?"

"We won't be eatin' turkey," Willie said, finding it hard to speak through his stiff lips. "What were you two walkin' around for like you was in a park?"

"Wanted to find out what the Krauts was a-doin'," Billy Bob complained. "I figured we had 'em on the run. That's whut the radio said. They're supposed to be whupped."

Charlie Delaughter suddenly grinned. Billy Bob could never understand strategy. "I guess they don't read the papers," he said. Charlie was the scholar of the 101st. He had been snatched out of a secure niche at Georgia Tech, studying to be an engineer, and thrust into the war. He had chosen the Airborne as being more romantic than a slogging foot soldier. Now he was having second thoughts about that. He shook his head sadly. "This is probably the last big push the Germans are going to make, Junior, and they can't win it."

"Why in the cat hair are they doin' it for, then?"

"Who knows? Hitler's got some kind of a wild notion, I think. Anyway, they're throwing everything they got against us. They won't win, but it makes it tough on us."

"I wisht they'd go pester somebody else," Billy Bob grumbled. He started to get up, but Willie reached out and dragged him back. "Keep your head down if you want to hang onto it." He got to his feet and crawled out of the hole, dragging his rifle out after him.

"Where are you going, Sarge?" Billy Bob asked.

"Lieutenant Stone came by. Said for our squad to move out."

"Move out where?"

"Over by that open field we held day before yesterday,"

"Well, dang!" Billy Bob exclaimed. "Why'd they tell us to leave there if we was goin' back?"

"Ours not to reason why, ours but to do or die." Charlie Delaughter had a bad habit of quoting poetry that grated on Billy Bob's nerves. He grinned now and said, "That's in a poem I read at college."

"I bet it was wrote by some dang-fool Yankee!"

"All poetry is written by Yankees, Junior. You rebels are too busy eating sowbelly and carrying on feuds."

"Come on, you two," Willie ordered. Heaving himself out of the foxhole and stumbling from tree to tree Willie made his way through what was left of the forest. He glanced back from time to time, making sure that Billy Bob and Charlie didn't get lost. He finally found Pete Maxwell standing behind a tree, eating a can of C rations.

"How can you eat that stuff, Pete?"

Pete was a slight young man from Los Angeles. His only interest had been surfing until he had been caught up in the machinery of war. He was the only soldier that Willie Raines had ever met who liked C rations. "I don't see how you do it, Pete."

"Why, it's good. Here. How about havin' some with me?"

"No, thanks. Come on, we're changing the line." He paused to listen to distant rifle fire, then asked, "Where are Rog and Chief?"

"Over there behind that ridge."

Willie looked in the direction that Pete indicated and frowned. "They're out in the open? They should know better than that."

"Well, it was Roger's idea," Pete shrugged. "He said he was tired of hiding behind trees." He grinned. "Chief told him that's why his ancestors whipped up on General Custer. Said if the fool had found some trees to hide behind he wouldn't have got all his men killed at Little Big Horn."

"Chief's right about that," Willie snapped. "Come on, let's find 'em."

As Willie led the three men through the trees, he was worried. Only five men were left in his squad, and Willie was determined not to lose another man. They had gone through training in the States together, had jumped behind German lines together on D-day, and had fought their way across Holland and France together. Willie had never had a brother, and these men were like brothers to him now. He'd never cared for poetry, but he liked the poem Charlie Delaughter had quoted once. Charlie said it was from one of Shakespeare's plays. He had explained that it was the speech that King Henry V gave to his small army before going into battle at a place called Crispin Crispan.

As they passed out of the forest into the open ground, Willie whispered the words of the poem that he knew, not speaking aloud, for he was somehow embarrassed about quoting poetry. He didn't know all the speech, but part of it seemed to have burned itself into his brain:

> Crispin Crispan shall ne'er go by,
> From this day to the ending of the world,
> But we in it shall be remembered—
> We few, we happy few, we band of brothers,
> For he today that sheds his blood with me
> Shall be my brother.

Somehow the words gave Willie Raines a fierce determination to bring the five surviving members of his squad safely through the war, no matter what it took!

Willie continued moving to his left. He heard the sound of someone singing and knew it had to be Roger Saunders. Saunders had a beautiful singing voice and seemed to know the words to all the latest songs from the States. This one was a ditty called "Pistol Packin' Mama," and the nonsense song sounded strange in the midst of the forest with death behind every tree—and overhead as well when the Stukas flew over.

Willie spotted the two soldiers standing in the open field as if they were in the middle of Central Park. He opened his mouth to call out to Roger when suddenly both soldiers whirled and threw their M1s to their shoulders. Willie was looking right down the barrels and managed to call out, "Don't shoot, you clowns—it's me!"

"Oh, is that you, Sarge?" Roger lowered the M1 and nodded. "I almost potted you that time."

"What a disgrace that would be, gettin' shot by a songbird. Who do you think you are, that singer all the girls are goin' crazy over?"

"Frank Sinatra? Well, he's good, too," Roger grinned. He was twenty-three years old, the oldest man in the squad, two years older than Willie himself. He was a New Yorker and a fierce fan of the Yankees baseball team. He was the only married man in the squad, and missed his wife Irene terribly. He wrote her every day, even knowing that there was no way to mail the letters from the spearhead of the army.

"What's up, Sarge?"

"Moving over to our left, Chief." Willie hated to reprimand any of his men publicly, but he was upset. "What are you doing out in the open, Chief?"

"Why, this paleface here got tired of trees." Lonnie Shoulders was a full-blooded Sioux and was never called anything but "Chief."

"You should know better than to listen to him."

"Oh, I *know* better," Chief grinned. He was a tall, strong figure with dark eyes and a coppery skin. "I just don't *do* better." He began stamping his feet on the ground and asked, "What's goin' on down the line?"

"The same thing that's goin' on here."

"Hey, I got a new one for you, Sarge," Roger Saunders said.

"A new what?"

"A new song. See how you like this one."

Roger began singing a song "All I Want for Christmas Is My Two Front Teeth."

Raines could not help but grin at the soldier. "Don't you ever worry about gettin' killed, Rog?"

"Nope. No time for that. Do you?"

"Well, it's crossed my mind," Willie said sharply. "Let's get moving."

Chief said, "Hey, Sarge, Roger and me liberated some grub. What say we build a fire and have some hot chow?"

Willie hesitated, then said, "OK, but first we dig in."

"Right!" Chief grinned. "I'll be in charge and be sure you guys do the digging right!"

"No need for anyone to dig," Billy Bob said. "We can use that there crater."

Willie turned to see the crater, and it looked good. He walked over to the large hole and stared at it. "It's big enough, but it's out in the open."

"Get loose, Sarge!" Pete Maxwell urged. "The Krauts ain't awake. I think they take siestas."

"That's *Mexicans* who do that," Charlie laughed. "But it's been pretty quiet, Willie. I think we'll have time to heat up some chow before we move on."

Against his better judgment, Willie nodded. "OK, but hurry it up. I don't like this spot." He moved out, his eyes darting over the terrain as the squad began gathering sticks for a fire. Climbing to the top of the low ridge, he stared at the wooded hills that rose in the west. Somehow they looked sinister, and he shook his head. "A bad place to get caught," he muttered. He turned and looked back at the squad, and almost called them to move on. But their voices were happy, and he forced himself to wait. "They need a hot meal, and we can move on when they've eaten."

· · ·

"This is good stew," Roger nodded. "You can get a job as a chef in Boston after the war, Chief."

The six men were sitting on the edge of the crater, eating the hot stew out of their mess kits. A pot of coffee was boiling in Pete Maxwell's helmet, sending a sharp fragrance to the soldiers. They were all laughing and prophesying when the Germans would draw back.

"I heard Patton is on his way with his tanks to relieve us," Pete Maxwell said, gulping down the hot coffee so fast he could hardly talk.

"Old Blood and Guts," Billy Bob said. "I wish he was here."

"Think he's as good as Stonewall Jackson was, Junior?"

"No Yankee is as good as Stonewall—and stop callin' me 'Junior.'"

Chief Shoulders nudged Willie with his elbow. "How about we get a leave when we whip these guys? Maybe in Paris."

"You'd scare them to death, Chief," Pete Maxwell said. "They're afraid of Indians."

Willie Raines sat back enjoying his stew. He had no idea what was in it, and he didn't want to ask the cook. It was hot, and that was all that mattered. But he was more pleased with the obvious pleasure the squad was taking in the break. These men had become his whole life, and as his glance moved from face to face, he thought again of the poem and the lines "we few, we happy few, we band of brothers." It pleased him, but he was nervous. He finished his stew and was about to order the men to finish so they could move into their new position when the quiet suddenly was split wide open by explosions on their left.

"Mortars!" Willie yelled. "Everybody keep down!"

Another explosion came from their left and then another from the right.

"They got us straddled!" Pete Maxwell yelled. "Run for it!"

But Willie had heard the sound of automatic weapons and knew that if they got up and ran, they'd be cut down. "Get in the foxhole!" he yelled, and the men fell into it headlong.

Willie tried to think, but he knew that Maxwell was right. The mortar squads had spotted them, and they were straddled.

To "straddle" a position meant that the Germans knew where they were. They were dropping shells to the left and to the right, with each mortar shell moving the mortar so that the shells fell inexorably closer to the target.

Willie knew that there was no way out, for each round was closer than the last.

"You guys keep clear." Willie grabbed the automatic rifle that Maxwell usually carried and got out of the hole.

"Where are you goin', Sarge?" Chief asked.

"Somebody's got to knock out that mortar squad." Willie leaped up and began running. He heard several voices calling on him to stop, but he ran full speed, but not in a straight line. Sudden shots rang out, and he saw a branch not five feet from his head clipped by a bullet and fall to the ground.

Infantry with covering fire, Willie thought and fell into one of the smaller craters. He huddled there enduring the cold but his mind working rapidly. *I've got to get that mortar! But how? I can't run straight forward against infantry fire. There are probably snipers there.*

While Willie stayed in the hole trying to think, the mortar continued to drop shells, and bullets were zipping all around.

Suddenly Willie was aware of a shape that had appeared to his left. He threw his rifle up, but a voice came, "Don't shoot, soldier. I'm with you."

The soldier who joined Willie in the crater was a lieutenant. There was nothing special about him except that he seemed very calm. He did not even bother to stoop down inside the hole but sat down on the lip of it. "It looks bad, doesn't it, Willie?"

"Do I know you, sir?"

The officer did not answer. He turned and looked over his shoulder. "The mortars are right over the ridge behind a small mound. You can't see 'em, but they're there. If you'd cut to your left, you can follow that line of trees and come up over the ridge. That way you can get to them."

Willie heard a singing of bullets and the explosions of the mortar shells and knew he had to do something.

"Are you ordering me to go, Lieutenant?"

"No. It's up to you, but your men back there won't make it unless somebody gets that mortar crew."

Willie Raines was a very ordinary individual. He was a good sergeant, but he had never been in a position like this. He had heard of suicide charges, and this seemed like one to him.

"What . . . what should I do, Lieutenant?"

The lieutenant turned toward him. His eyes had a strange glow, and he seemed calm—so calm that it was unnatural. He said quietly, "Save your men, Willie."

Willie Raines did not hesitate. Leaving his automatic weapon on the ground, he pulled one of the grenades from his belt and jumped up. He ran to his left where the officer said there was no covering fire, but still he heard bullets whistling by. There were plenty of trees to take cover behind, and the noise of the mortar shells exploding seemed dim and far away. All the same, however, he knew he had little time to save his squad.

Emerging from the trees, he ran up a slight hill, and when he got to the top and glanced to his left he saw the mortar squad. They were dropping mortar shells into the steel tube and shifting it after every fire to straddle the target.

Willie started running again. He pulled the pin from the grenade. Bullets were whistling around him, but he ignored them. He knew he had to get close, and as he did, he saw the mortar squad turn. One of the men was scrambling for a rifle, and Willie knew he had little time. He heaved the grenade with all of his might and with the same motion pulled the pin on the second one and threw it. Just as he did, something seemed to explode. It seemed to be inside his head, and he was aware of a blinding display of sparks much like holiday fireworks. His last conscious thought before the sparks and the fire display faded was, *I sure do hate to die on Christmas!*

Chapter
TWO
❧

B en Raines looked up from the colored brochures that littered his coffee table and grinned broadly. *"Euphoria,"* that's what I have. I don't believe I've ever had euphoria before."

Clara Munson, Raines's cleaning lady, was running the vacuum cleaner over to his right. The ancient cleaner made more noise than a B-17, but Clara had acute hearing. She looked across the room at Raines and bellowed, "You got *what?*"

"Euphoria," Ben shouted back.

"It ain't catchin', is it?"

"I wish it were. No, euphoria, my dear Clara, means 'a feeling of well-being or elation.'"

Clara gave the vacuum cleaner another push, considered this, then shut the machine off. "Why are you feelin' so good?"

"Because, dear lady, I'm going to Spain."

"Nothin' over there but Spaniards."

Ben Raines laughed and stretched broadly, reaching for the ceiling and arching his back. "I suppose that's true

17

enough, but then there are Germans in Germany and Frenchmen and frogs in France."

Clara sniffed and went back to vacuuming. She was a heavyset woman of fifty, usually cheerful, but with stretches of depression when she did not win at Bingo.

Raines sat back down and began studying the travel brochures. All of his life he had wanted to go to Spain for some reason, and now he was going!

Suddenly a sound from the television reached him, and he looked up to see that a game show was on. "I can't stand game shows!" He clicked the remote and suddenly there was Jimmy Stewart and *It's a Wonderful Life*.

Raines quickly clicked the remote again, and Clara, who had stopped to watch the screen, said, "Why did you turn that movie off?"

"I can't stand *It's a Wonderful Life*."

Clara was scandalized. "It's my favorite movie!" she protested, her face screwed up as if she had bitten into something sour. "It's *everybody's* favorite Christmas movie."

"Clara, it's not true."

"What do you mean it's not true? It ain't supposed to be *true*. It's a movie. You read true stuff in newspapers."

"Not always, Clara," Raines said wryly. "I wish everything you read in the papers were true, but unfortunately that's not the way things are."

"Well, ain't that an awful thing to say!" Clara snorted. "Here you write for a newspaper, and now you tell me they don't tell the truth."

"Clara?"

"Anyways, movies ain't true—not like the Bible. They're just supposed to make you feel good."

Ben knew he shouldn't argue with Clara, for he'd never won an argument with her. "That movie shows life the way life is not."

"What do you want, one of these movies where they chop people up with chain saws? That's *true* enough. People really do those awful things."

"No, I don't want a chain saw movie, but I don't want *It's a Wonderful Life*."

"It's a movie that makes you feel good."

Raines always found it impossible to argue with Clara Munson. She was incapable of reason. He had announced once to his boss, "My cleaning lady thinks with her feet."

"*It's a Wonderful Life* makes people hope for miracles," Ben said finally, knowing that would not help with Clara.

Clara turned to face Raines. The fact that he was her employer never caused her to modify her behavior one fraction. "And what's wrong with hoping for miracles?"

"I don't believe in miracles, Clara."

"Didn't I tell you how my first husband nearly died but God healed him, how he got up out of that hospital bed and walked when all the doctors said he would die? God healed him. It was a miracle."

Raines grinned but refused to argue. "I'll tell you about a miracle, Clara," he said quickly. "I'm going to Spain and have a month of sunshine and no writing! Now that is a real miracle!"

"You just want to go watch them poor bulls get killed, that's what."

"I'm not going to a bullfight."

But declarative sentences had never influenced Clara. She had bullfights on her mind and could not get them out. "You're just awful, Ben Raines, that's what you are. Them poor bulls never hurt nobody."

Knowing he was making a mistake, Ben said, "Look, Clara, do you know anything about those bulls?"

"I know they get kilt."

"Those bulls are taken care of all their lives better than any animal on earth. They're very valuable. Their owners have special herdsmen to take care of them. They have the best grass, good water. If they get sick they have a vet."

"They still get kilt."

Raines threw up his hands. "They have one bad afternoon in their whole life. I've had as many as twenty bad afternoons in one month."

"So you'd rather be one of them bulls and get kilt with a sword?" She pronounced the *w* in the word *sword* persistently.

"I think I would. It beats what I've got."

"You ain't got no gratitude. That's what's wrong with you."

"Well, I'm going to Spain, and I'm grateful for that and it's a miracle."

Clara Munson sniffed. "That ain't no miracle. That's just leavin'. You arranged it all your own self. A miracle is somethin' God has to do. It ain't something you can do yourself."

"Well, if it's not a miracle, it's close enough for me, Clara."

Ben Raines vowed for the five hundredth time never to argue with Clara. He went back and studied the brochure. It featured a picture of a flamenco dancer, a dark-haired, dark-eyed beauty with her hands over her head, clicking her castanets and smiling seductively.

"Spain, here I come—a miracle, no matter what Clara says!"

• • •

Although Christmas was nearly a month away, there were the beginnings of decorations and signs of the holiday spirit at the Veteran's Hospital. As Ben entered the lobby, he saw a Christmas tree being erected by two sturdy women and stopped long enough to say, "You're a little bit early, aren't you?"

"Never too early for Christmas." The older of the two women gave him a wink and said, "Merry Christmas to you."

"Bah humbug," Ben said and saw the two stare at him. "Just kidding. Imitating Scrooge."

"Scrooge who?"

"Ebenezer Scrooge from *A Christmas Carol*."

"Is it a movie?"

"As a matter of fact, it is. But before it was a movie it was a novel by Charles Dickens."

"I never seen it, but if he says 'Bah humbug!' about Christmas, it couldn't be a good movie."

"Well, I beg your pardon. Go on with your decorating, ladies."

Ben made his way to the elevator, and when he got inside he saw a hand-printed sign: "Wanted: Someone to be Santa Claus."

Ben stared at it, then muttered, "Here's my chance. If I really wanted to have a miserable Christmas instead of just my usual not-good Christmas, I could dress up in a red suit with a pillow for a stomach, come down and be Santa Claus to the veterans."

The elevator stopped at the third floor, and Ben got off and walked down the hall. He saw that already there were Christmas cards pinned to the bulletin board where important bulletins were usually kept. When he reached his father's room, he started to turn in, but Mabelene Williams, a large black woman in a white uniform, was coming out. "Hello, Mabelene."

Nurse Williams stared at him. "Well, you did come—at last."

"I've been real busy, Mabelene."

"I'll bet you have."

For some reason Mabelene felt it was her calling in life to shame Benjamin Raines for not coming to see his father more often. She was usually successful, for Ben already had a guilty conscience about the matter. Every year he made resolutions to come and see his father at least once a week, but somehow it never worked out that way. "I'm going away for Christmas, but I promise you, Mabelene, I'll come every week before Christmas."

"You won't be here for our Christmas party?"

"No, I'll be in Spain."

"Well, I hope you enjoy yourself." Mabelene's eyes went all flinty, and she had more to say, but Ben didn't want to hear it. He had heard it all before, and besides, he didn't need to carry a guilty conscience with him to Spain. It probably was against the law to do such a thing. He said, "Merry Christmas, Mabelene," and ducked inside the room. His father was in his wheelchair, and his head was tilted to one side. He was sound asleep. His mouth was open, and he looked helpless and vulnerable.

Ben stood there uncertainly and then took a chair, moving quietly. He knew his father wouldn't mind being awakened, that he always wanted to talk, but what was there to talk about? Desperately, Ben had tried to interest himself in the affairs of the Veterans Hospital. When his father had first come here four years earlier, he had been more faithful, but coming to visit his dad had become a drudgery that he hated.

Ben sat and studied his father, and as he did, uninvited thoughts came trooping into his head. He wished heartily that there was a lock on the door of the mind—that he could shut things out that had no business there. But there was not. He had tried everything. It irritated him that he was an intelligent man but could not control his thoughts.

Sitting there with the pale sunlight streaming through the window, Ben regarded his father, Willie Raines. In Ben's mind William Raines had always been a failure. He had volunteered for the army and had been so terribly wounded at the Battle of the Bulge that he could never again do heavy work. He was unskilled at anything, and during

Ben's formative childhood years the family had moved from one place to a cheaper one throughout the meaner streets of Chicago.

Ben thought about how many times during his teenage years his father had been unable to work, and Ben had had to struggle to bring in what income he could. This meant that he was not able to participate in sports, at which he had been rather good, and even after all these years it took all the strength he had to keep the resentment back.

The sleeping man stirred, coughed, and suddenly reached out with his hand as if trying to grasp something. He mumbled something in his sleep, and his face twisted. But then he relaxed, and Ben leaned back in his chair. He thought of the years he had spent at the newsstand on Thirteenth Street. His father had finally managed to buy into a newsstand, but it had been Ben who had had to keep it running. It was an outside newsstand, covered with plastic and canvas when it was closed, but Ben had sat there many weary days, through snow and sleet and ice and blistering summers, while the other boys were out playing ball.

Harsh, bitter memories stirred within Ben, and he had a sudden impulse to get up and flee the room. He was not a Christian, but he had strong notions of right and wrong, and one of these notions was that it was wrong for him to despise his father for his failures. When he tried being logical, it had come out something like, *You should have been born to a rich father. Your mistake was being born to a poor daddy. Somehow it's all his fault.* He realized the ludicrous logic that lay here, but now as he sat there he tried desperately to think of other things.

"Why, hello, Son."

Snapping back to planet earth, Ben made himself smile and stood up. "Hey, Dad. How you doing?" He put his hand on his father's shoulder and felt how fragile the man was. He seemed to be nothing but skin and bones, but the blue eyes that had turned up to him were lively.

"I'm glad to see you, Son. You're looking good."

"So are you, Pop."

Willie Raines's face was shrunken. The flesh was faded, and though he had been an attractive man in his youth, he had lost all that. "Clark Gable had better watch out, eh?"

"Yeah, that's right."

Ben pulled the chair over and began searching for conversation topics. His father liked baseball, but baseball season was far away. Willie cared little for football, so that was out. Finally Ben began edging toward the subject that he dreaded. He talked about his work and how he hadn't had a vacation in nearly three years.

"You really need to take some time off, Son. You work too hard."

"Well, Pop, I think you may be right about that. As a matter of fact, I've got a good opportunity here, but it would mean I'd be out of town during Christmas."

Willie's eyes did not change. "What is it, Ben?"

"You know how I always wanted to go to Spain?"

"No, I didn't know that. You never told me."

"Well, I've always wanted to go there. I don't know why. It just looks like a nice place to visit, especially during our winters here. So, I finally got some time off, and there's a special on with one of the travel agencies. Trouble is, I'd be gone dur-ing Christmas. I wouldn't be able to come and be here."

"Well, you can come and see me before you leave. Take lots of pictures," Willie smiled. "When you get back you can show 'em to me and tell me all about it."

"Why, sure, Pop. I could do that, couldn't I?"

Relief swept over Ben like a wave. "Well, that's what I'll do then. I wanted to talk to you about it first."

"You remember," Willie said, "what good Christmases we had when your mother was alive?"

"I sure do."

"That woman loved Christmas. Sometimes she'd start in October getting ready for it. When we first got married I thought it was silly, but I got so I looked forward to it."

Ben remembered the Christmases then. They had been bright spots in his life, and the two talked about those times.

"She believed in angels, too."

"She sure did."

"Well, I guess I do, too."

Anxious to change the subject, Ben said, "I'll tell you what. I'll have a special Christmas dinner, turkey and dressing and all the fixings, brought in just for you. I'll have Clara bring it in. She's always cooking for her family. She'd be glad to."

Willie Raines looked up, and there was a gentle smile on his lips. He had never once complained about his condition in all the times that Ben could remember.

"Well, that'll be fine, Son. You take lots of pictures of Spain, and when you come back, maybe there'll be some turkey left for you."

• • •

Whistling off-key as he always did, Ben went through the trash in his office. He hated to throw anything away, but now was the time, and his wastebasket was stuffed with old business and worthless mail that seemed to come more and more often.

Ben could hear the sound of Andy Williams singing Christmas carols from an office down the hall. Since his mother had died he had paid little attention to Christmas, but he always liked Andy Williams. At least he could carry a tune.

"Hello, Ben."

"Hi, Sal. I just came to clear out a few things."

"How's your dad?"

"I was there this afternoon. He's about the same."

Sal Victorio, the editor of the paper, looked more like a Mafia hit man than an extremely able editor. He was literate to an incredible degree, but he always looked as if he were about to pull out a gun and shoot someone. He had mentioned once to Ben that his grandfather had been in the Mafia, but his father had gotten away from that life. He had sent Sal all the way to Harvard University and was as proud of his son as if he were the president.

Ben said, "I haven't been on a trip in a long time. I've got to buy some new luggage."

Sal removed the cigar from his mouth, stared at it for a moment, then jammed it back in. He always kept a cigar exactly in the center of his mouth, and it looked now like a gigantic fuse attached to some monstrous bomb. It also smelled like burning rope, since Sal did not believe in wasting money on good cigars. "You heard about Sam?"

"You mean *our* Sam?"

"That's right. Sam Benton."

"What about him?"

"He had a heart attack."

For an instant Ben thought he had misunderstood his boss. "Was it serious?" he asked finally.

"It could have been worse." Sal shrugged his beefy shoulders. "The doc says he's going to be all right, except he's gonna have to have a bypass."

"But he always eats right, and he does those exercises. He's a health nut."

"Looks like that doesn't make much difference. He didn't even have a pain. He went in for an annual check-up, and the doc did an EKG. Told him he was either gonna have a heart attack or he was having one right then, and Sam never felt a thing. It made him kind of mad, but he's got to have that surgery."

"Sorry to hear about that. Right here at Christmas, too. Be tough on his family."

"It's gonna be tough on you, too, Ben."

For a moment Ben stared at his boss, and then a suspicion began to rise in him. "Now wait a minute, Sal!"

"You're the man."

"What are you talking about?"

"You're a smarter guy than that. You'll have to fill in until Sam can come back."

Disappointment mixed with anger began to stir in Ben Raines. "You've been promising me a vacation for two years, and I've got everything set up. I've even got the ticket."

"I'm sorry, but that's just the way it is. By the way, you'll have to do the Christmas story."

The paper had one big Christmas story as a tradition. It was something that Sam Benton usually did and that Ben had always said he couldn't do.

"I've been looking forward to this vacation for six months."

Sal took his cigar out then lifted his eyes toward Ben Raines. "Sam took over for you when you had mono for a month."

There was no answer for that, Ben knew, nor was there any way out of this. He was going to have to stay in Chicago, and he was going to have to write the Christmas story, and he would have to put up with all of the phony Christmas trappings that went on every year, but there were some things a man had to do. He straightened up and tried to force a smile. "Why sure, Boss, I'll take care of it."

Chapter
THREE
෨ఞ

"D o you really think angels look like that, Dad?"
Willie Raines twisted his head around and looked at
the picture on the wall to his left. It was a picture that Ben
was familiar with, for it had been in his parents' room as long
as he could remember. The painting showed a young boy and
girl about to step into a dangerous chasm, but over them hovered a bright shining winged figure, his hands outstretched
as if to protect them.

To Ben the picture had seemed somehow *wrong*, even when
he was a child. He'd stared at it often, and wondered if God
really cared enough to send an angel to look after wandering
children. As he'd grown older, he liked the painting less and
less—though he never mentioned his feeling to his parents.

"Well, I don't know, Son. I expect God's got different
kinds of angels. One of them might look like that, but others
might look like something else. Funny thing, every time an
angel appeared to someone in the Bible, the first thing he'd
say was, "Fear not."

"Why do you suppose they said that?"

"I guess they were pretty spectacular. In the book of Revelation an angel appeared to the apostle John, and he fell down and began to worship him."

"What'd the angel do?"

"Why, he said, 'Don't do that!' or words to that effect."

Ben looked at the picture and remarked, "You've had that picture a long time, haven't you?"

"Ever since I got out of the army. Your mother saw it for sale on the street and bought it for me. I remember that day just like it was yesterday," he said.

Ben suddenly remembered his mother as she had been when he was young, and a wave of loss touched him. "You still miss Mom, don't you?"

"Every day of my life, but I'll see her one day soon." Willie smiled gently, and a light touched his faded blue eyes. "You know, Son, people talk about people who die being *lost*, but I don't see it that way."

"Why not?"

"Because if you know where something is, why, it's not lost, is it?"

"No, I guess not."

"I know where your mother is, so she's not lost. I like to think she's waiting for me to show up." Willie laughed suddenly, adding, "I was always late for things, and your mom was always on time. So I'm a little late, but I'll catch up with her pretty soon."

Remarks like this made Ben Raines uncomfortable. He himself had given up on religion when he was no more than twelve years old. He knew his father, however, was a staunch believer in the Bible, and he quickly changed the subject.

"I've got some good news, Dad. I'm not going to be gone for Christmas."

"What about that trip to Spain?"

"I decided not to go. Too much work to do at the office."

Willie Raines studied his son thoughtfully then asked, "You're not giving up your trip just because of me, are you?"

Ben didn't like to lie, but this was the time for it. He grinned and said, "I've got to fill in for a friend, but that's OK. It'll be good to be here with you."

"I hate for you to miss your trip."

"Spain will be there. It's not going anyplace. One thing I have to do is to write the annual Christmas story."

Willie Raines brightened up then and asked, "Christmas story? What's that?"

"Oh, you know, Dad. Every year the paper has a long story on some aspect of Christmas."

"Oh, yes, I remember. It was always the best part of your paper, I thought."

"Maybe I could write something about the Christmas you had at Bastogne," Ben said. Instantly he saw something change in his dad's face. "What's the matter, Dad? You don't want to talk about that?"

Ben's dad had talked very little about his service during the war. Ben had grown curious a few years prior and had gone to the War Department and dug out the citation that went with the silver star that his father had won. It impressed him mightily, more than anything his father had ever done, but now he saw that there was some hesitation in his dad. "That might be a real good thing. People need to remember what you guys did in the war, and it was Christmas, wasn't it?"

"Yes, it was."

"I read the citation. That was quite a stunt you pulled off, charging into that rifle fire and then tossing those grenades and wiping out that mortar squad. I remember when I was a kid I was prowling around in your chest of drawers, which I shouldn't have been doing," he grinned.

"You always were a nosy little guy."

"I remember once I found something I thought was chocolate candy in a little tin box. I ate 'em all."

Willie Raines suddenly laughed. "I remember that. Turned out to be Ex-lax, a pretty effective laxative."

"Well, I don't want to talk about that," Ben said quickly. "It wasn't so funny at the time. Anyway, I found your medals in there, your silver star and the purple heart. I remember asking you to tell me about it, but you never would."

"I guess I just didn't want to talk much about that time."

"Hey, you *should*, Dad. It's something to be proud of. Isn't there some way we could get a story out of that Christmas?"

A silence fell over the room, and Ben waited patiently. His father, he well understood, was not a man who spoke easily about matters that were close to him. Finally Willie shifted in his chair and said, "It was a bad time. Cold as I can ever remember. I used to tell your mother during cold times here in Chicago, 'Well, it's not as cold as it was at Bastogne.' She always laughed at that."

"I'd like to hear the story from you, Dad."

"You really would?"

"Sure. Like I say, it's something you should be proud of."

Willie chewed his lower lip thoughtfully, ran his hand over his hair and then said, "All right. If that's what you want."

Willie began speaking slowly and Ben did not interrupt. He listened carefully to the entire story, and finally when Willie ended, he took a deep breath. "That's some story, Dad."

"I haven't told it to anybody in a long time."

"Lucky thing for you, and the rest of the guys in the squad, that lieutenant was there. I wonder how he knew how to get at that mortar emplacement."

Willie Raines gave his son a searching look. "There's one thing about that story that's not in the citation."

"What's that, Dad?"

"I didn't know that lieutenant."

"He wasn't the lieutenant in your company?"

"I'd never seen him before in my life, Ben, and I knew most of the officers, by sight at least."

"Maybe he was from another company."

"When I woke up in the hospital, the first thing I wanted to know was how were the guys in my squad. They were all OK. Then I started asking about the lieutenant, but nobody knew anything about him. I did everything I could to find out, but they thought I was just hallucinating. But I wasn't, Son. I can remember that officer just as clear as I can remember anything in my life."

"He was probably a replacement."

"No, he wasn't. I checked everything that could be checked." Suddenly Willie looked over to the picture of the angel, and when he turned back there was an odd look in his eyes. "I think he was an angel."

"An angel! Come on, Dad, you don't believe that."

"I thought about it a long time, and that's what I've decided. God decided that He was going to save our squad, and so He sent an angel down to tell me how to get at that mortar emplacement. I know you don't believe in things like that, Ben, but I do."

For an instant Ben could not answer. He could not pretend to agree with his father, for Willie knew perfectly well he didn't believe in angels or anything else very much. On the other hand he hated to destroy his father's dream, so he took the best middle ground that he could.

"Well, anything's possible, I suppose." The look in his dad's eyes made him uncomfortable, so he got up and said, "I'll be back tomorrow, but one thing we're going to do is plan a great Christmas celebration right here. I'll bring the turkey and dressing when the big day comes."

Willie Raines smiled. "That'll be mighty fine, Son. I'll look forward to it."

As Ben left the hospital he continued to mull over their conversation. The story of the angel he dismissed at once. *Could have been a dozen ways some officer could come in there. A replacement. Somebody lost from his own unit. Or maybe Dad just dreamed it, imagined it. I'll have to talk to the doctors about it.*

• • •

Ben Raines spent most of the afternoon walking the streets of Chicago. It was something he often did when he could not get a handle on a story or a piece of writing. Usually something would come. It was not exactly like in the cartoons where a lightbulb goes off over a character's head, but it was sort of like that. A thought would come, and when he meditated on it, thought about it awhile, it would begin to grow and swell like a tree puts out branches. That was the way the story was filled in.

But this time nothing came—absolutely *nothing*. Finally he went home, fixed himself a TV dinner of chicken and rice, then sat down in his recliner and watched part of a football game. He didn't care much about the game. Who won wasn't important to him one way or another, so he dozed off.

When Ben woke up, his mouth was dry and he felt confused. Opening his eyes, he started to get up out of the chair and suddenly realized that *It's a Wonderful Life* was on. It was the scene where Clarence had saved Jimmy Stewart from committing suicide and was explaining to him how important his life had been.

More than once during the next hour Ben nearly turned the movie off. He had seen it more than once, but somehow this time he felt compelled to watch. Finally it got down to the last of the movie, where all of the people that Jimmy Stewart had helped during his life came to his rescue, and Stewart realized that his life had not been in vain after all. Others had gone ahead of him and made more money and become famous, but his life had counted, too.

And then it suddenly came to Ben: *I'll write a story about Dad and the people whose lives were changed because of what he did at Bastogne.*

The idea was as clear as crystal, and he got up out of the chair and began walking back and forth, excited by the idea. *I'll find those men that were in that foxhole with him, the members of his squad. Shouldn't be too hard to trace them. He probably knows where some of them are. Then I'll find out what they've done since the war. Some of them may not still be alive, but some probably are.*

As always when Ben Raines got an idea, he ran away with it. He could not stop his thoughts. They seemed to tumble over themselves. His thinking was all intertwined with *It's a Wonderful Life*, but he thought, *That's just a movie. Real life's not like that.*

He fixed himself a cup of coffee, sat down at his computer, and began typing preliminary notes. He discovered at once that there was a problem.

"It won't be like the movie," he said aloud. "Some of them may have wound up in the penitentiary, but I'll tell the truth." Another idea came, and he typed rapidly.

"'The Angel of Bastogne.' That's what I'll call it. Has a nice ring to it." Suddenly, as sometimes happened, he got a sentence that would do to begin the piece with. The first sentence of any writing was always important, whether a newspaper story, a novella or a full-length novel, and this one came to him. And when he had typed it, he stared at it and read it aloud:

"We would all like for stories to have happy endings, but most of them don't."

Pleased with this, Ben wrote rapidly, jotting down ideas, and as he did, the last line of the story came to him. He wrote it down, then read it aloud:

"I'd like to believe in angels, but that's not for most of us. Don't wait for a Christmas angel to take care of you."

A troubled thought then drifted into his mind. *Dad won't like this story the way I'm going to write it. He always was kind of a romantic, optimist. Always thinking things would turn out all right, but it just doesn't happen like that. I can't tell him the angle of the story, but I'll have to get the names of the men whose lives he saved.*

Going over to the window, Ben looked out. It was a cold, gloomy day and yet he could hear the sounds of a Salvation Army band coming faintly. He moved to one side and saw them down there, only five of them—two trumpets, a saxophone, a tuba, and a big bass drum. None of them were particularly adept, but they were doing their best. Another three members of the band, all dressed in the army uniform, were singing away. Ben could make out the words faintly:

> Hark! The herald angels sing, "Glory to the new-
> born king;
> Peace on earth, and mercy mild; God and sinners
> reconciled."
> Joyful, all ye nations, rise, join the triumph of the
> skies;
> With the angelic hosts proclaim, "Christ is born in
> Bethlehem."

The words of the old song drifted up, bringing with them the aroma of memories long buried in Ben Raines's mind. He listened until the army finished its song, and then he turned away, but fragments of the song stayed with him. *Glory to the newborn king, Christ is born in Bethlehem.*

The words, which he'd heard all his life, seemed to echo though his spirit, touching old memories. He suddenly remembered his mother singing that song with her eyes filled with light—and he knew he'd give anything to see her again.

Chapter
FOUR
༜

A stiff wind threw the snowflakes across the highway in front of Ben. Dancing like tiny ballerinas, they were so dry they did not even stick to his windshield. The sky was pale gray, and the sun had hidden itself, but the weather report had said there would be no winter storms coming in.

Reaching over to his side, Ben flipped open the composition book he kept his notes in and held it up. He scanned the five names that he had written there. Willie had not had the addresses of two of them, but it had been no trouble to get them from the War Department. He had never met any of the men, but he familiarized himself by scanning the list.

1. Charlie Delaughter
2. Roger Saunders
3. Billy Bob Watkins
4. Pete Maxwell
5. Lonnie Shoulders

Ben's thoughts centered on these five men. His father had told him that the rest of the squad had been killed or wounded by the time they had been surrounded at Bastogne.

But these five were the ones Ben would feature in his story. As the car sped along, he realized he had mixed emotions. He was still upset about getting done out of his trip to Spain, but this had the makings of a good story. It could be a good piece of writing, and that always excited Ben. Glancing down at the bottom of the page, he saw an amplification of the names. Beside Charlie Delaughter was a note: Survived the war but died in 1972. Delaughter had at least one child, a daughter named Charlene. Dr. Charlene Delaughter. Practices in Evanston, Illinois.

This had been a break, for Evanston was within driving distance of Chicago. Ben had found Dr. Delaughter's name in the phone book. He had not been able to speak with her, but a nurse had called back and informed him that Dr. Delaughter would see him at five o'clock on Wednesday. He had quickly taken the appointment, and now as he made his way toward Evanston, his mind was already preparing itself for the story he would write. Willie had told him that Charlie Delaughter had been one of the best men he had ever known and that he was the one that should have gotten the medal. "He never quit. He never refused a tough job. He never complained. That was Charlie. I still miss him, Son. . . ."

. . .

Finding a parking place at St. Charles Hospital was not particularly difficult. Night was closing in now, and the wind drove tiny fragments of sleet and flakes, stinging Ben's face as he got out of the car. The two-inch layer of snow coated the parking lot and made crunching noises as he walked toward the front of the hospital. He shivered beneath his lightweight coat, drawing it closer about him as he climbed the steps.

When he entered the building, he saw an elderly woman sitting at the desk marked Information. Advancing to the desk, he nodded and the woman smiled pleasantly, saying, "Good evening. Can I help you?"

"I have an appointment with Dr. Delaughter."

"She's probably operating. That would be on the second floor, and the elevator's right over there."

"Thank you very much."

"Merry Christmas."

"Merry Christmas to you."

Ben had never learned how to handle such phrases as "Have a nice day" or "How are you doing?" He felt obligated to respond, and for the meaningless "Have a nice day," he'd made it a habit to merely smile. Once when a man had asked him, "How you doing," Ben had made it a point to tell him in great detail. He had shocked the man, who'd muttered an excuse before Ben finished giving him an update. Ben learned to just say, "Fine."

As to the holiday greeting "Merry Christmas," Ben knew he couldn't say, "Bah humbug!" so he surrendered and simply said the words.

The hospital was not busy, and Ben felt uncomfortable, as he always did in hospitals. He could never explain this feeling. Strangely enough, he had never been a patient in a hospital, not one day in his entire life, but everything about them frightened him. The smells, the uniforms, the broken bodies being wheeled on stretchers up and down the halls, some of them looking already dead.

On the second floor, he went to the desk where a man and a woman were laughing and drinking from paper cups. The woman was young and attractive, and the man was overweight and had a flushed face.

"Yes, sir, may I help you?" the young woman said.

"I am supposed to meet Dr. Delaughter."

"She's in surgery. I'm afraid you'll have to wait. There've been a couple of emergencies."

The heavyset young man nodded with his head. "Waiting room is right down the hall."

"Can you get word to Dr. Delaughter that I'm there?"

"Sure, we'll tell her," the man said.

"Is there any place to get something to eat?"

"The cafeteria closed early. Sorry about that."

Ben did not want to leave the hospital for fear he might miss Dr. Delaughter. "What about a coffee machine?"

"I'll get you some," the pretty young nurse said. She got up, disappeared down the hall, and the young man studied Ben. "Got someone in the hospital, buddy?"

"No. Not this hospital."

"We got a full house. We had to call Dr. Delaughter. Kid got thrown out of a car."

"She's a surgeon?"

"Pediatric surgeon mostly. The best, too. If I had a kid got hurt, I'd want to have Doc Delaughter take care of her if I could."

That sounded like a lot of *ifs* to Ben, but he was interested in finding out all he could about the woman. "She been on service here long?"

"I guess so. I just came a month ago myself. I come from Georgia. It's cold up here. I wish I was back there."

Ben listened as the young man extolled the glories of Georgia and the South over Illinois and the North until the nurse came back. "Here you are, sir."

"Thanks."

"Here's some sugar and cream."

Ben took them, smiled his thanks. "You'll call me when Dr. Delaughter's free?"

"Yes, and I'll let her know you're here," the nurse smiled.

Ben nodded, walked down the hall, and entered the waiting room. A middle-aged couple looked up as he entered. They were sitting close together and holding hands. Both of them had tense looks on their faces.

"Hello," Ben said. They greeted him but said nothing. Ben sat down and sipped at his coffee. It was pretty bad. Ben had often said that the worst cup of coffee he ever had in his life was very good, but this almost made him decide to change that statement. It tasted something like he imagined old tar would taste. For the next hour and a half Ben sat and fidgeted in the chair. He made the rounds of the tables beside the chairs, going through the magazines. Most of them were for women: *Redbook*, *Ladies' Home Journal*, *Cosmopolitan*, *Better Homes and Gardens*. Ben scanned through them, trying to find something that interested him and wondered with some irritation why they didn't have a *Sports Illustrated* or a *Popular*

Science. Didn't they know a man had to endure the miseries of a waiting room as well? Finally he gave up, went down to his car, and got the notebook.

After returning to the waiting room, he sat there making notes, trying to recast the story without a great deal of success. The story would come from the people, and he hadn't met any of them yet.

"Do you have someone in surgery?"

Ben looked up quickly and saw that the middle-aged man had spoken to him. "No, I don't. How about you?"

"Our daughter," the man said. He could not control the slight tremor in his voice. "She's only three."

"I hope it's not serious," Ben said. He made his living with words, but in situations like this, he could never find words that had much meaning. He dreaded funerals, for what can one say to the survivors? He understood that people should go, and they should say something, but such things were a torment to him. He hesitated before asking, "What happened to your daughter?"

The man started to speak then had to stop and clear his throat. The woman, who looked to be in her early forties, said quickly, "She was with some friends at a party and was thrown out of a car. The door popped open."

Ben tried desperately to think of something that would bring a faint encouragement to the couple. He saw the pain and the fear written across the faces of the pair and made the inane remark, "I'm sure she'll be all right." Then he realized he should have said, "I hope she'll be all right," but it was too late to change it.

"Dr. Delaughter is doing the surgery," the woman said, and hope came to her eyes. "We know she's in good hands."

"Is Dr. Delaughter your doctor?"

"More or less. She's a pediatrician, but she does mostly surgery now."

"What's your daughter's name?"

"Her name's Angela. I wanted to name her Angel," the man said, "but Mary here talked me out of it."

"Angela is a fine name. I suppose it means angel in Spanish."

"Yes. I think so," the man said. "That's what she is, an angel."

"You have other children?"

"No. I had five miscarriages. We married late, so she's all we have."

Once again a feeling of helplessness touched Ben Raines. *I'd hate to be a doctor and bring bad news to a couple like this,* he thought. He tried to think of something comforting, and nothing came to him. Fortunately, at that moment, a woman in the garb of a doctor with a stethoscope around her neck stepped in. At once the two got up and rushed to her. "Is she all right, Doctor?" the woman cried.

"She's going to be fine."

Ben watched and listened carefully as he studied the woman. She was tall and had ash-blonde hair. He put her age at somewhere around thirty-five. The hospital garb did not conceal the fact that she was still a shapely woman, and it interested him how the two clung on her words. He listened and felt a gust of relief, as if Angela were his kin.

"It wasn't nearly as serious as we thought at first. She'll have to stay here for a few days, but she's going to be just fine."

Ben listened as the two poured out their thanks to the doctor, and then when they hurried away to be with their daughter, he arose and said, "Dr. Delaughter?"

"Yes." The doctor turned to face him. "You must be Ben Raines."

"Yes, I am."

"I'm sorry to be so late, but—"

"It's all right. I'm just glad things turned out for the little girl."

"It was a little bit more difficult than I let them know, but they are very fragile, and I didn't want to disturb them." She had gray eyes, or blue or green. It was hard to tell in the harsh light of the waiting room. They were large and well-shaped and were studying him carefully. "Are you hungry?" she asked suddenly.

"Starved."

"Then let's go get something to eat."

"I don't want to put you out."

"It never puts me out to eat. Do you like Italian?"

"I like any kind of food. I even like airplane food."

"Not really?"

"No, but Italian is fine."

• • •

Luigi's was exactly what an Italian restaurant ought to be. It had the atmosphere of Italy somehow, and the sharp spicy aroma of garlic and other good things saturated the air. The owner, none other than Luigi himself, looked very much like a working member of the Mafia except he had a gracious smile. He greeted Dr. Delaughter warmly and seated the two at a table. "We don't see you enough, Doctor."

"You certainly don't," Dr. Delaughter smiled. "I'd weigh two hundred pounds if I came as often as I want. What's good tonight, Luigi?"

Luigi spread his hands in a pure Italian gesture, overly dramatic. "When you get something not good at Luigi's? It's *all* good!"

"Surprise us then."

"I will do that. You justa' wait!"

As the owner left, Ben said, "Dr. Delaughter?"

"Just Charlene will do, or most of my friends call me Charlie. I hate it, but they do it anyway."

"Charlene then," Ben grinned. "And, as you know, I'm Ben."

"I know quite a bit about your dad but nothing about you."

"You never met my father, did you?"

"No, but I have letters that my dad wrote to my mother when he was in the war. You'd be surprised at how important Willie Raines was to my dad."

"I'd sure like to see those letters."

"Of course. I can't give them to you, but you can make copies."

"That would be great."

They waited until the meal came, talking in generalities about the weather and Chicago and trying to get each other's measure. The meal, when it came, was outstanding. It started with freshly baked bruschetta with red peppers and garlic in olive oil for dipping and a large plate of antipasto with the meats thinly sliced and the black olives very salty. Next came a small salad with thinly sliced tomatoes, onions, black olives, grated cheese, slivers of garlic served with a light, spicy dressing. Finally Luigi brought out a large platter with small helpings of spaghetti and meatballs, veal parmesan, lasagna, and a four-cheese ravioli, plus a basket of piping hot garlic bread.

Luigi hovered over them, opening a bottle of wine and instructing them on how best to enjoy the meal. When he left, Charlene Delaughter said, "He treats his customers like I like to treat my patients, gives them his full attention."

"How long have you known you wanted to be a doctor?"

"Since I was three years old."

Ben grinned. He liked this woman. She was direct. He liked her looks, too, for her oddly colored eyes held some sort of laughter but also mirrored some ancient wisdom. Her eyes were wide-spaced, and as he looked into them, he noticed that they seemed to have no bottom. Her complexion would have been the envy of many teenage girls, and he could not help but notice the ripe and self-possessed curve of her mouth. She had that assurance that most doctors have, and she also had a gift of listening that many doctors did not have. He found himself telling her about the story he intended to write.

". . . so, what I would like to bring out in the story is the fate of the five men that Dad saved by wiping out that mortar."

"I think that's a wonderful idea for a story." He watched as she took another bite, not a small one but a large one, and chewed it thoughtfully. When she swallowed, she frowned for a moment, then met his eyes. "You know, Ben, I always thought your father was the greatest man in America."

The remark caught Ben by surprise. "I never thought of my dad like that."

"Well, to me he is, because, according to all the authorities, if he hadn't taken out that mortar emplacement, my dad would have died, and I wouldn't be here. So to me he's the greatest hero in American history."

"I'd like for Dad to hear that, and it'll certainly go in the story."

"You put it down just like I said it. Dr. Charlene Delaughter insists that Sergeant William Raines is the greatest hero in American history."

"I'll do it."

Charlene sipped the water that she chose over the wine and said, "It's like science fiction, isn't it?"

"What do you mean, Charlene?"

"Haven't you ever read any time-travel stories? You know, when they send someone back in the time machine they warn them, 'Don't change anything. If you kill somebody, you might kill my ancestor and I wouldn't be here. Don't even kill a butterfly.' Who knows what would happen?" She laughed and said, "I never believed those things, but somehow it's like that. What your dad did changed everything for a lot of people. There were at least five families that wouldn't have existed if he hadn't gone after that mortar squad."

"I never thought of it like that."

"I think it's like that movie. Have you ever seen *It's a Wonderful Life*?"

Ben blinked suddenly. "Yes, I have. Who hasn't?"

"That's right. Probably the most watched movie in America. I've always loved it."

Ben stared at her and when she saw his expression, she said, "What's the matter, Ben?"

"I never liked the movie."

"You didn't like *It's a Wonderful Life!*" Charlene exclaimed. "Why, you must be a communist!"

Ben forced himself to laugh. "Nothing that bad. It's just that it's so perfect, and life just doesn't work out like that."

Charlene studied him carefully, and then she said quietly, "Sometimes it does, Ben. God's still in control. I think He had His eye on me and some other people when He used your dad to save those men."

The same sense of embarrassment that Ben felt when his father mentioned religion suddenly rose in him. He dropped his eyes and could not speak.

"What's the matter? Does that embarrass you?"

"I . . . a little bit, I guess."

"You don't believe in God?"

Ben suddenly found it hard to answer her question. "I believe, somehow, there is a God. There has to be. But I have trouble believing that He cares. I don't see how as a doctor you can. You're bound to see terrible things, especially in your line. Little children who die needlessly."

"I feel all of that, but I have to believe in the Lord. He's all I have to put the world right. Of course," she added quickly, and a serious look framed her face, "we're living in enemy-occupied territory. But one day it won't be. One day Jesus will be on the throne, and all evil will be locked away. That's when life will really begin. Wouldn't you like that, Benjamin Raines?"

"I'd like it a lot, Charlene. I just can't get a handle on it."

• • •

It had been a wonderful meal, and Ben hated to see it end. He had taken notes about Charlene, facts that he could work into the story. He had cautiously told her the focus of the story, and she had been excited about it. She was one of those buoyant, enthusiastic Christians who believe everything he didn't, but there was nothing phony or hypocritical about her. He knew that about this woman.

"I guess I'll have to go," he said. "Got a lot of traveling to do."

Something seemed to be working in Charlene's mind, and she looked up and said, "I'm a very forward woman. I guess you've noticed."

"Not really. Why do you say that?"

"I'm about to shove my way into your business. That's my spiritual gift, meddling."

"Meddle away," Ben said, wondering what in the world she was talking about.

"I'm taking some time off for Christmas. Haven't had a vacation now in a long time."

"That was my plan, too. I was going to Spain," Ben said ruefully. "Now I'm not. A friend of mine had a bypass."

"I'd like to help you with the story."

"Are you a writer along with being a doctor?"

"Oh, nothing like that. But I'm a pilot, and I have a plane. If you'd trust me, we could fly together to meet the families of the men that were with our dads in that foxhole at Bastogne. I'd like to meet them."

"Some of them might not be alive, you know."

"I know, but I'd like to meet their families. I've wanted that for a long time."

"Why, of course, that would be wonderful as far as I'm concerned, if you'd let me pay the expenses."

"Nope. It's on me. My Christmas gift to the famous writer Benjamin Raines."

"Hardly that," he said. He suddenly grew excited. "That would just be perfect! They're scattered all over the country. It would be exciting."

"You're not afraid to fly?"

"Well, it's not my favorite thing."

"Are you afraid to fly with a woman?"

Ben suddenly laughed. "You must be a feminist."

"I'm feminine. Men usually would prefer that their pilots be male."

"I don't feel that way at all. I can be just as petrified with a male pilot as I can with a female pilot. When I get on a plane, I try to forget about who's flying it and the fact that I'm flying." Ben hesitated, then said evenly, " Charlene, maybe I ought to throw one thing at you."

"What's that?"

"I think you already know. I don't believe in very much."

Charlene was watching him silently. "I know that," she said quietly.

"I don't believe in Santa or the tooth fairy—or in Jesus." Ben waited for her to react, and he halfway expected her to withdraw her offer or at least to be upset.

"You're not too old to believe; nobody is. But that's not a requirement. I think it'd be a good way to spend Christmas. Think what a great Christmas gift you'd be giving these people!"

"What gift?" Ben said, confused by her words.

"You're going to write this story, and when they read it, they'll read about the men that fought for us. They'll be heroes. They're already heroes to their families, I'm sure, but now other people will know their stories. It's a great gift, Ben."

Ben suddenly felt warm. "I never thought of it like that, but as long as we know where we stand, all right."

"Good. When are you going to visit the first family?"

Ben reached over and squeezed her hand. "As soon as you can fly me there, Doc."

Chapter
FIVE
❦

The plane, which had flown level and steady for the past two hours, suddenly dropped like a stone. Ben made a wild grab, seeking something to hold on to, and felt the weightlessness as the aircraft dropped. He let out a small, frightened sound and then felt the pressure on his bottom as the plane leveled off again.

"Air pocket."

Ben turned to see Charlene studying him. Humor danced in her eyes which, at this moment, seemed to be as green as the waves of the sea.

"You did that on purpose," Ben said accusingly.

"Not really. We just hit an air pocket. It happens all the time. Nothing to worry about."

"I'll find something."

Ben slowly forced himself to relax and glanced down at the earth far beneath. They were high over Montana now, not far from the landing field at Billings, or so Charlene had informed him. They had left Evanston early in the morning and had stopped once for fuel and to get something to eat.

"Haven't you ever flown in a small plane before, Ben?"

"No. Just a big jet." He looked down at his hands and saw that his fists were clenched tightly together. He forced himself to straighten his fingers out and cleared his throat, saying defensively, "You're insulated on a commercial flight."

"That's right. You don't have any sense of being in the air after the takeoff. It's like being put in a big box. You get in the box and a few hours later you get out of the box." Charlene shook her head, and he saw she was smiling at him. "This is the real thing. You have the sense of flying."

Ben looked down at the earth again and shook his head. "I'd rather be in the box. As a matter of fact, every time I get on an airplane, I have the impulse to ask for a general anesthetic. I just want to get from one place to the other."

"That's an awful way to live, Ben."

"What are you talking about?"

"Just getting from point A to point B is no fun. It's the journey that's important."

The steady hum of the twin engines had lulled Ben, a time or two, until he felt drowsy. He knew that Charlene was a good pilot, for he had carefully checked on her reputation at the airport. All the mechanics and other workers there said she was outstanding. One of them, the manager of the airport, had nodded confidently. "Why, she could be a commercial pilot if she wanted to. You can't say better than that."

Ben gave Charlene a cautious glance. She was wearing a pair of pleated jeans and a loose-fitting wool sweater. Her hair was pulled back carelessly and tied with a black ribbon, and she looked right somehow flying the plane. "I guess I'm just a coward," Ben said.

"No. We're all afraid of something."

"What are you afraid of?"

"Snakes."

"What kind of snakes?"

"Any kind. If it doesn't have legs and goes along the ground, I'm petrified. We'll probably see some in Montana. Then you'll have to take care of me. Are you afraid of snakes?"

"No. Never was. As a matter of fact, my nickname was Snake when I was growing up."

"Where'd you get a nickname like that?"

"A bunch of us guys were out camping. A rattler made a strike at one of the guys, and I reached out and grabbed him by the tail and flung him off into the woods."

Charlene turned and her eyes were enormous. "You grabbed him by the tail?"

"Well, that's what the Bible says to do."

"What are you talking about? Where does it say that?"

"My mother used to read me Bible stories. This was in the book of Exodus, I think. God told Moses to throw his rod down, and it became a snake. Then God told him to pick it up by the tail. I always thought that was odd. It looks like the wrong end to me. The front end's still free to do the business."

"I remember that story. Your mother was a Christian?"

"Yes."

The plane rose when a thermal updraft caught it, and Ben waited until it leveled out again before he shrugged his shoulders. "She's all the argument I ever need for Christianity. I have lots of doubts myself, but she didn't. Neither does Dad."

When she didn't speak, he added thoughtfully, "I guess I'd be better off if some of their faith had rubbed off on me."

"Why, it will."

"You sure about that, Charlene?"

"'Train up a child in the way that's right, and when he grows old, he will not depart from it.'"

"That's in the Bible, is it?"

"Yes, it is. I believe it, too. You'll come home one day." She suddenly peered down and said, "I think that's Billings over there. Don't get nervous when I set this crate down."

• • •

While Charlene made the arrangements with the airport to keep the plane, Ben rented a car, a year-old Taurus. Ben had instructions about how to get to the Shoulders Ranch, but it turned out to be more difficult than he had thought. It was really located thirty miles out of Billings and off the main road. They stopped once at a gas station, and the owner, a tall thin man with bright blue eyes, exclaimed, "Why shore I know where Lonnie Shoulders lives! You go down that road and turn off two miles before you get to the water tower."

Charlene suddenly laughed. "You mean we have to go to the water tower and then come back two miles."

"Well, there ain't much of a turnoff to mark it. You can see the water tower, and just keep your eye on your right and you'll see a fence. Go through the gap in the fence. You have to get out and open the gate. Lonnie don't keep it locked. Watch out for that big red bull of his though. He's a thumper! You know Lonnie, do ya?"

"Not really. He was a friend of my dad's," Ben said.

"Fine fellow. Got a good family, too."

Ben paid for the gas then got back in the car and started the engine. As he sped down the highway, he said, "Sounds like Lonnie Shoulders has got a good reputation."

"Don't you know who he is?"

"Lonnie Shoulders? Why, he was in the army with my dad and your dad. That's all I know."

"You don't keep up with rodeoing much, do you?"

"No. Not really. I often wondered why anybody would want to do it. It seems to me it's a horrible way to make a living."

"I guess they just like it. But, anyway, Lonnie Shoulders was All-Around Cowboy for three years in a row when he got out of the army."

"That's good, is it?"

"It's like winning the World Series in baseball or the Heisman Trophy in football. Lonnie won Best All-Around three years in a row. Can't get better than that."

"How do you know about all this?"

"Oh, my brother rodeoed awhile. I'd go with him. It was fun."

"What does your brother do now?"

"What my husband did. He was a pilot in the navy."

It was the first time Charlene had mentioned her husband, and Ben had not felt like asking. "Your husband was a flyer?"

"Yes. Top gun or close to it."

"How did he . . . "

"How did I lose him? It was a flying accident, of course. Not his fault. He was training a younger pilot who made a bad mistake, and they both died. We were very close, my husband and I."

"And your brother's a flyer also?"

"One of the best. He doesn't fly jets, though. He flies helicopters."

"I'm sorry about your loss."

Charlene did not answer for a time, and when he turned to study her, he saw that her lips were set. "We had a good marriage," she said. "There's not a day goes by that I don't think about him."

"You didn't have children?"

"No. We never did."

"Any other family?"

"My mother's living. She has a condo in Pensacola. She and my brother get together a lot. I go when I can."

"Look, there's a big billboard."

"Wonder what it's selling."

They got closer, and Charlene began to laugh. "I don't believe that!"

In big, bold letters, the sign said, PLEASE DO NOT FEED THE JACKRABBITS!

Ben laughed. "Somebody spent a lot of money on that sign. Must have a real sense of humor."

Suddenly Charlene said, "Look, there's a gate!" She pulled up and peered forward. "There's the water tower."

Ben looked and shook his head. "Can you see that far?"

"Why, that's not far at all. You probably need glasses."

"Well, I haven't got eagle eyes like you. I'll get out and open the gate."

"Watch out for that bull."

There were no bulls in sight, but Ben saw some large cows grazing. The road wound its way around small hills, and when he got back in the car, Ben said, "I don't know much about ranches. I think about ranches in the movies and on TV—the Ponderosa and John Wayne. Probably not very true to life."

"I think it's pretty hard work. I thought for awhile about being a vet, but I went another way."

"How did you decide to become a surgeon?"

"Oh, I didn't. First I was just going to be a pediatrician, but I found out that I had a knack for surgery so I went that way."

"How did the girl do who you operated on the day we met?"

"Doing fine. Makes me feel pretty good to be able to help like that."

She spoke of her work with pride, and Ben said, "It makes my little job seem kind of piddling, writing stories."

"We all have something to do in this world. We just have to find out what it is. God wants me to operate on children. He wants you to write stories."

"I'm not sure about that."

She did not speak, but a few minutes later she said, "There's the ranch."

Ben sat up straighter in the seat, and as they crested a small hill, he saw the ranch. It was surrounded by trees, and several barns with outbuildings were behind it.

"What a nice-looking ranch!" Charlene exclaimed.

Ben looked around. "Seems lonesome to me. I'm a city boy."

Ben drove up a circular driveway to the front of the house. As they got out a tall man, somewhat lanky and wearing a black Stetson low on his forehead, came out of the door. He had a coppery complexion and black eyes that glittered. His face was lined, and his high cheekbones proclaimed his Indian blood.

"You folks lost?"

"No, sir, I don't think so. We're looking for Mr. Lonnie Shoulders."

"That's me."

"I'm Ben Raines and this is Dr. Charlene Delaughter."

Instantly Lonnie squinted. "Have we met before?"

"No," Ben said, "but you know our fathers."

"You're not Willie Raines' boy, are you?"

"That's me."

"Willie talks about you in his letters," Lonnie said.

It was the first time that Ben had known his father had kept in touch with his old army buddies. "I hate to barge in on you like this."

"No bargin' to it. Come on in. We'll have something hot to drink. It's colder than a well digger's toes out here."

"That's not the way I heard the expression," Charlene said, "but I could use some coffee or hot chocolate."

"We got both. Come on in and meet my bunch."

Inside, the house was decorated with the heads of deer and antelope on the walls. The floors were hard pine, and there was a warm atmosphere. A fire burned cheerfully in a huge rock fireplace, and over the mantle were three trophies.

Charlene walked over and looked at them. She turned and said, "I saw you the night you rode Dynamite."

"Did you now? You must have been a wee thing."

"I was only five, but I remember it. I still have the program. My brother took me. Larry Delaughter."

"Old Larry! You're his sister? He was a plum good bull rider. What's he doin' now, Doc?"

"He's a flyer for the navy."

"Do tell! Well, he was some cowboy. He could have done well if he had stayed with it."

A woman entered, and Lonnie Shoulders said, "This is my wife Dove. Dove, this is Dr. Delaughter, and you'll be surprised at this fella. He's Willie Raines' boy, Ben."

Dove Shoulders' hair was almost as black as Lonnie's but more streaked with silver. Her eyes were wide and expressive, and at the introduction she came forward at once and put her hand out to Ben as a man would do. Ben took it and felt the strength of it despite her age. "I'm so glad you came," Dove said. "I guess you know in this house we hold your dad pretty high."

Ben could not answer for a moment. Somehow the story was not working out as he had thought it might. First a pediatric surgeon and now a prosperous rancher, three-time All-Around Cowboy!

"Mama, these folks need somethin' hot. As a matter of fact, why can't we warm up some of that barbecue? You folks eat barbecue?"

"I do," Charlene said. "I'm a glutton for barbecue."

"You come to the right country for that, Doc. Come on in the kitchen. That's where we live anyhow."

The two followed the older couple into the kitchen, where they were at once given huge mugs filled with fresh, scalding coffee off the stove. As they sat and drank it, Ben found himself explaining why he had come. "I'm going to do a story about your squad, Mr. Shoulders."

"Stop right there. It's just plain Lonnie, but the guys all called me 'Chief.' What kind of a story?"

"About what happened to your squad at Bastogne."

Lonnie was quiet. He had huge hands worn rough by work, and the large cup looked small in them. "I think about them boys a lot. Especially your dad, I guess." He looked up and grinned. "He's mighty proud of you, Ben."

A sense of shame seemed to burn into Ben Raines at that moment. He wished he had paid more attention to his father, and somehow the idea that his father was proud of him was embarrassing.

"Well, I'm not the man he was."

It was the first time in his life Ben had ever thought that, much less said it aloud, but he had found two people that saw in his father something he had missed all of his life.

"How is Willie? He'll never tell me a thing about how he is except I know he's in the hospital."

"He's gone down pretty fast, I'm afraid, Lonnie."

"I hate to hear that."

Dove Shoulders warmed up barbecue, and neither Ben nor Charlene argued at the huge servings they got. They also had fried potatoes and creamed corn along with fresh-baked rolls.

As they ate, Lonnie asked question after question about Willie, and Ben was embarrassed that he could not tell him more.

"What about your family, Dove?" Charlene suddenly asked.

"Well, you shouldn't have asked because I was gonna tell you anyway. We have three children, two girls and one son."

"He looks like me, worst luck," Lonnie laughed. "But on the other hand the girls look like their ma, so better that way than the other way around."

"Our son's been a missionary in Iran for the past eight years," Dove added.

Both Ben and Charlene stared at the couple. Finally Ben cleared his throat. "That's pretty hard, isn't it? I mean, they don't welcome missionaries over there."

"No. You have to go as something else. David's a scientist. Got him a Ph.D. in botany. He's over there tellin' 'em how to grow better crops. So he has to do his witnessing like that. Can't have churches or anything."

"That's a very dangerous world he's in, especially for Christians," Charlene said. "I know you're very proud of him."

"I'm as proud as a cat with two tails," Lonnie Shoulders nodded vehemently. "He's a good boy, David. He always was.

All I ever done was rodeo, and here is this boy of mine goin' over preachin' the Lord Jesus to people that need to hear it."

Dove then left the table and soon returned with an apple pie, and, despite their protests, both Ben and Charlene ate small pieces.

Ben took notes copiously about the family, took snapshots of them with his Nikon, and got them to sign releases for using them.

"I've often wondered why you didn't write about your pa. He sends us your pieces, you know," Lonnie said. "I keep 'em all."

Ben felt inordinately pleased at this. It made him feel a little bit better.

"You know," Lonnie said, "if it wasn't for your dad, none of this would be here. I'd have been buried over there somewhere around Bastogne. I'd never have married Dove, we'd never have had our children." He shook his head thoughtfully. "And there wouldn't have been no David to go to Iran and tell them people that Jesus died for them." A thought crossed his dark eyes, black as obsidian, and he said softly, "You know, Ben, it's kind of like your dad went over there himself!"

• • •

The lights of Billings glittered below as the plane gained altitude. Ben had said very little after they had left the Shoulders property. He had returned the car while Charlene checked the plane, and now he sat thinking over what had happened.

"What are you thinking about, Ben?"

"I was thinking about the Shoulders family. They're fine people. You know?"

He broke off suddenly and shook his head.

"What is it, Ben?"

"Something I don't like to admit."

Charlene lifted the plane higher with the touch of her hands and said quietly, "Sometimes confession's good."

"I know, but it's hard, too." He was silent for a time and then said, "The thing is, Charlene, I've always been ashamed of my dad. He never seemed to do anything. He came home from the war and tried several businesses, and finally we wound up with a little newsstand. He got sick, and I had to take care of it most of the time. I guess I've always resented that."

"It must have been hard on a young boy."

"I didn't make many excuses for my dad. I always thought he could have done better."

Charlene Delaughter suddenly reached out and put her hand on Ben's arm. She squeezed it and said, "I don't know your father, but if people like the Shoulderses think so much of him, I'd venture to guess that your dad did the best he could."

The words cut Ben Raines like a razor, for he had had exactly the same thought. He could not think of a single word to say in his own defense, so he sat there silently as the plane moved rapidly through the darkness.

Charlene Delaughter held the Cessna on course, but her mind was on the man who sat beside her. She turned and studied his profile, not certain of how she felt about him. He was an attractive man, of that she was sure—but there seemed to be something troubling him.

He's a man without a star.

Charlene had read of the ancient navigators who steered their frail ships across trackless seas by the light of one dim star. She'd always admired such men, and now as she cast another glance at Ben Raines' profile, she thought, *He's lost and afraid—and he can't admit it.* She said nothing, but knew that somehow God had put the two of them together for some purpose more important than a newspaper story.

Chapter
SIX
❧

T he weather is getting worse, isn't it?"

"Yes, quite a bit." Charlene leaned forward and peered out into the dark clouds that seemed to wrap the plane as in a blanket. "I don't like to fly in stuff like this."

"Maybe we ought to set down somewhere," Ben said. "Could we do that?"

"That's what I'd like to do. Let me see if I can contact the nearest airport. Probably have to be a regional airport."

Ben sat bolt upright, trying to hold the plane up by his willpower while Charlene called several airports. Finally she turned to him and said, "There's a small airport about five minutes from here. The tricky part is getting down in this stuff. You can't see anything until you're right on the ground."

"I don't guess you can make an instrument landing."

Charlene shook her head. "No, that's for big jets with all kinds of equipment that they have at big airports. Here it's just ooze down a little bit at a time and hope you don't encounter anything nasty like a TV tower or something like that."

It irked Ben that he could do absolutely nothing to help. He liked to be in control of things, and here he was as helpless as a baby. His life was completely in the hands of this woman who sat beside him. He studied her covertly, noticing that while she was alert there seemed to be no sign of fear. That eased his mind somewhat—but not completely.

"Here we are," Charlene said and seemed to expel her breath. "Now we can see a little something."

Indeed, they had dropped below the cloud cover, and although a freezing rain was falling steadily there was visibility enough to see the ground. "How will you find the airport?"

"Look for it. It's the only way, but it shouldn't be too hard."

Five minutes later Charlene said, "Look! There's the strip right there."

"Looks awfully small."

"Probably was a private airport that they designated as a regional airport, but there'll be plenty of room for us."

Charlene brought the plane in perfectly, and as soon as she taxied up to the hangar and shut the engine off, Ben expelled a sigh of relief. "Well, I don't know about you, but I'm glad to be here."

"I was a little bit worried myself. There's not much we can do about the weather. We may have to stay here all night and maybe tomorrow. Do you have anybody you need to call?"

"Not really."

"Well, I do. I have to have someone go in and take care of Tammy."

"Tammy? Who's that?"

"My cat. Come on. Let's see if we can find a place to stay."

The two got out of the plane and found nobody inside the hangar. "Service with a smile," Ben said. "What do we do now?"

"We'll call a cab, and he can take us to a motel for the night. There's a small town over there somewhere about five miles away according to the map. They probably will have a Knotty Pine Motel."

• • •

The motel was called the Royal Motel, but there was little royal about it. It consisted of eight small, identical cabins, and they had five vacancies. They took a cabin apiece, and Ben asked the sleepy-eyed clerk, "Could we get a meal? Where's the best place to eat around here?"

"The Elite Café. It's the best place. It's the worst place, too." He grinned and said, "It's the only place that'll be open this time of the night. Don't eat the steak."

"What's wrong with it?"

"They're awful." The clerk was a young, pimply-faced man with the beginnings of a beard that was a mistake. *He probably grew it,* Ben thought, *to hide his complexion and to give him a little maturity, but it seems to emphasize both the complexion and the immaturity.*

"Where is it?"

"Right down the street there, three blocks, and it's right on the highway. You can't miss it. It'll have a sign outside: 'Mom's Place.'"

"You know what Hemingway said about that, don't you?" Charlene said. "He said, 'Never play cards with a man called Doc and never eat at a place called Mom's.'"

"Well, we got candy bars and cheese and crackers in the machine."

"I guess we'll try Mom's," Ben said.

The two left the motel, and as they walked along, Ben saw that the town itself basically straddled the highway. It was, more or less, a strip mall with a few side streets. "I'd hate to live in this place," he said.

"Probably some pretty nice people here."

"But it's so dreary."

"Some of them probably think it's a great place to live. They'd hate it if you made them live in Chicago or any other big city."

"Well, there's Mom's Place. I hope the Board of Health has been keeping a close watch."

Mom's Place was a storefront café with the lights shining out into the gloomy darkness that had fallen now. When they stepped inside, the warmth came at them with a rush, and Ben said, "Well, it smells good."

Mom's Place consisted of one large room with a door leading to the kitchen. There were ten tables with tablecloths that didn't match, nor did some of the chairs. A radio was playing country western music, and Ben grinned wryly. "What a break. We get music with our dinner. I don't think there's going to be a hostess. How about right over here?"

The two sat down at a table that was covered with a red and white checked tablecloth. The toothpicks were in an empty Tabasco bottle, and the salt and pepper shakers were in enormous aluminum containers. An oversized bottle of Tabasco sauce completed the condiments.

Three of the tables were occupied, two of them by couples and one by a solitary man who looked like a truck driver. All of them had turned their attention to the newcomers, and the truck driver called out, "Mom! Customers!"

The swinging door to the kitchen opened, and a short woman, round as a beach ball, came out. She was in her late fifties, and her hair was drawn back in a bun. She wore no makeup and no ring. The sleeves of her dress came down to her wrists, and the hem of her dress was well below her knees. "Good to see you. Pretty cold out tonight."

"It's getting worse, I think," Ben said.

"You two stayin' over?"

"The weather got us, so we'll have to stay until it clears up."

"Well, hope you enjoy your stay." The woman had a moon-round face and large brown eyes, also round. She was pleasant-looking and said, "What can I bring you?"

"Do you have a menu?"

"There it is on the wall."

Ben and Charlene turned to see a chalkboard with the selections available. Ben studied them and said, "I guess I'll have the pork roast."

"We got potatoes and carrots with that and fresh baked bread."

"I'll have the same," Charlene said quickly.

"What'll you have to drink?"

"Coffee for me—decaf," Ben said.

"Me, too. No cream."

"Won't be long. Just set right there."

"I'll wait until you get here," Ben grinned. He saw the woman was amused by his remark.

"There ain't no place else to run to in this town—if you're hungry, that is." She turned and walked away, and Ben said, "Seems like a pleasant lady."

"I think she's a Pentecostal lady. Notice that bun?"

"Sure did. It's got her hair so tight her eyes look slanted."

They both sat there until Mom brought the food back. The serving of meat was enormous, as were the vegetables. The butter was in a round mound instead of being in small squares and wrapped in tinfoil. "Made this butter myself. You can't get that in the big city."

"You sure can't, and that bread smells delicious," Charlene said.

"You want to bless the food, or do you want me to do it for you?" Mom said, looking down at them.

Ben was suddenly amused. "I guess you'd better do it for us, Mom. You've probably had more practice than I have."

The woman bowed her head and began praying loudly enough for everyone in the café to hear it. "Lord, bless this food and bless this man and this woman. May they be washed in the blood of the Lamb, saved, sanctified, and filled with the Holy Ghost. In Jesus' name. Amen."

Charlene looked up with a broad smile. "That was a wonderful blessing. Thank you, Mom."

"Are you a sanctified girl?"

"I sure am."

"What about you, Sonny? You walkin' in the light?"

"I guess you'd call me a searcher."

"Well, the Bible says, 'They that seek me, they shall find me.' The good Lord said that Himself. So, you go ahead and eat, and I'll be here if you want refills."

"Thank you," Ben said. "It looks delicious."

"That was some blessing," Ben said as he began to cut the pork roast. He put a bite in his mouth, and his eyes opened wide. "This is terrific!"

"It sure is. She spiced it up somehow or other."

"The vegetables are good, too." They ate hungrily, and Ben glanced over at Mom who had brought coffee out to refill the cups. She carried it in an old-fashioned aluminum coffee pot that looked like it would hold a gallon. "There aren't many women like her around these days."

"I think not. They're almost an endangered species." She picked up the huge mug of coffee, sipped it, and said, "What kind of woman are you looking for, Ben?"

"Looking for? What do you mean?"

"Well, you don't intend to die a crusty old bachelor, do you?"

"That's possible. To tell the truth, I don't really understand women."

"Well I'm glad you admit it. Women can be dangerous to a man. You know," she said as humor flickered in her eyes, "there was a poet named Graves who wrote about a girl who could fade the purple out of cloth and tarnish mirrors with her look."

"Must have been some woman."

"I think she was. Graves said she could walk between two men and if no appropriate prayer was said, one of them would die."

"I'd like to meet that gal."

The dinner was pleasant, and they lingered over it as long as possible. "I hate to go back to that motel room."

"So do I. The lonesomest place in the world is a motel room all by yourself—unless it's a Greyhound Bus Station with lots of people." Charlene said, "I bet Mom's got some good pie. Let's buy one and take it back to the motel with us. We'll stay up and watch whatever's on television and eat pie all night."

"What if she doesn't have pie?"

"Mom always has pie. You wait and see." She raised her voice and said, "Mom, do you have any pie?"

"All I got left is apricot, apple, and peach."

"Could you fix us one in a paper plate that we could take with us?"

"I sure can. Which kind you want?"

"What do you like, Ben?"

"Peach sounds good to me. My mom used to make peach pies."

"Peach it is, Mom."

Mom disappeared and came back shortly with a pie covered with aluminum foil. "This ought to put some meat on your bones," she said. She put the pie down, and Ben pulled out his billfold. "How much do I owe you?"

"How much you think it was worth?" Mom smiled. "You know, in our church one time our preacher said, 'Put in what God tells you to, and if you got a need, take out what God tells you to.'"

Both Ben and Charlene laughed. "Did you have any money left in that offering?"

"Shore did. Best offering we ever had. I guess ten dollars ought to cover it."

Ben put down fifteen dollars and said, "It was delicious. We'll probably see you for breakfast in the morning."

"Well, I'm cuttin' back on my breakfast, I'm afraid. I won't have anything but pancakes, eggs, ham, grits, red-eye gravy and biscuits."

"Well, life is tough. We'll just have to put up with it as best we can," Ben said. "Good night, Mom."

"Good night, and you keep a-searchin' for the Lord, young man."

"I will, Mom."

The two walked out into the cold, wet night and hurried back to the motel.

"Let's go in my cabin. I think they only get the network, but there's bound to be something on we can watch if it's only the news."

The two went into Charlene's room and put the pie down. Then Ben went off to see if he could locate some coffee. The young clerk said, "Sure. I keep coffee on all night. Come and get it any time you want it. No charge."

"Thanks," Ben said and hurried back. He saw a look of light dancing in Charlene's eyes, and she was smiling. "What are you laughing about?" he said.

"You're going to love the movie."

"How do you know?"

"They just told what it was going to be. Guess?"

"Why, I have no idea. I hope it's not one of Stephen King's horrors. I can't stand those things!"

"Oh no. You're going to love this, Ben. *It's a Wonderful Life.*"

Ben suddenly began laughing. "I cannot get away from that movie!"

"I don't think any of us can. It's part of Americana. Well, sit down and we'll have our first slice of pie and coffee."

The two sat down and watched the movie. During the course of it, they ate small slices of pie. There was no way to heat it up, for there was no microwave, but it was delicious in any case.

"I don't understand why this movie's so popular," Ben said at one point. "It's not the best acting in the world, although it's pretty good. I like Lionel Barrymore especially. Old Man Potter, he is really a tough case, isn't he?"

"I think it's popular because people want life to be good. They want the underdog to win."

"Well, the underdog usually gets stomped."

"You know what? This is a Godless movie."

Ben had been sipping his coffee that had grown tepid. "What do you mean, 'Godless'?"

"I mean nobody goes to church. Nobody says anything about the Lord. It's a world without God."

"Well, there's Christmas."

"It could have been Columbus Day. There's a Christmas tree, and that's it. There's none of the meaning of Christmas woven into it. It's a nice, moral tale without God in it."

"I never thought of that," Ben said. "I'll bet you don't like that."

"You're right. I think Jesus Christ is the only answer to our problems. I like to think about the day when He'll come back to this earth and everything will be set right. Did you ever stop to think how it would be if Jesus were the king of all the earth? There wouldn't be any prisons in heaven."

"Nor lawyers, I hope," Ben grinned.

"No. No lawyers. And there'd be one judge. I don't really know what heaven's going to be like."

"I don't like the idea that most people have. You sit on a pink cloud strumming a harp. I'd get bored out of my skull."

Charlene leaned back and closed her eyes and was silent for a moment. "Whatever heaven's like it's going to be exciting."

"You really believe that, don't you?"

"Yes, I do."

"I'm glad," Ben said suddenly, "and I hope you always will."

"Ben, can I tell you about myself, about how I became a Christian?"

"Why, sure you can."

Ben listened as she spoke for a long time about how she had found the Lord when she was an adolescent. "I had a hard time because almost none of the girls in my school, nor the boys either, were Christian, and they made fun of me. I took a Bible to school in those days, and that really set them off."

"I don't think that'd be permitted today. The ACLU would hear about it and try to stop you."

"Unfortunately, you're right."

Charlene talked for a long time, and finally the movie ended.

"Well, end of my testimony and end of the movie."

"It's a wonderful testimony, Charlene." Ben got up and said, "I'll give you the rest of the pie."

"No, I'd burst if I ate anymore. I'll look forward to that breakfast tomorrow. You can't get grits very easily in Chicago, but I'll bet Mom's are good." She got up and put out her hand. "Good night, Ben. It's been a good day. God was good to get us to this place safe."

"Yes, He was."

Suddenly he asked the question that had been on his lips more than once but which he had always managed to avoid. "You loved your husband very much, didn't you?"

"Yes, I did. I miss him every day."

"Do you ever think you'll find another man that means so much to you?"

Charlene thought for a moment. She had a way of thinking over questions that made them seem important. "It wouldn't be the same," she said, "but it might be richer in some ways. You know what they say, you can't step in the same river twice. If I married again, I'd miss some things that my husband and I had, but I'd discover some different things. Why are you asking? Am I a candidate?"

Ben did not laugh. "I've always felt like I've missed something without having a companion. You'd make any man a good wife."

The two were standing only a few feet apart, but each was vitally aware of the other. Ben noticed that Charlene's shoulders made a straight line, and not for the first time he noticed a sweetness in her lips and in her bearing. Something rash and timeless brushed against them both. He struggled with his desire to embrace her. "You know you have the power to stir me, Charlene."

"Any woman can do that."

"No. That's not true."

Bright color stained her cheeks, and Charlene held him with a glance half possessive. Her presence was like a fragrance, like a melody, coming over a great distance.

"You'd better go," she said.

"Are you afraid of me?"

"No. Maybe of myself. Good night, Ben."

"Good night."

He stepped outside and closed the door, and for a long time Charlene Delaughter stood staring at it. She thought about this strange man whose life had suddenly touched hers, and something stirred within her. Turning slowly, she began to prepare for bed but knew she would stay awake for a long time thinking of this night and this man.

Outside in the darkness, Ben Raines looked up into the sky and could not see a single star. *Seems like there'd be at least one star.* The darkness of the heavens depressed him, and he hurried to his room to shut out the thoughts that came to him, regretting that he had not reached out to touch Charlene when he'd had the chance.

Chapter
SEVEN
&

D ad, I'd like for you to meet Dr. Charlene Delaughter. Charlene, this is my dad, William."

"I'm so happy to meet you, Willie. I'm Charlene."

Willie Raines smiled and put out his hand. When the tall woman standing before him took it, he said, "I think I see some of your dad in you, Miss Charlene."

"People always said I resembled Dad."

"Well, you two sit down. I want to hear all about your trip, and I want to hear about your dad. We were really close when we were in Europe."

"I know. I brought a whole stack of his letters with me that he mailed from there. Some of them by the old V-mail. You remember them?"

Willie took the packet tied with a black ribbon, and after he had loosened it, he picked up one of them. "I had forgotten about these. Brings back old times."

"Dad was a great letter writer."

"I remember that. He was always scribbling away, even when the bullets were flying overhead."

Charlene smiled and shook her head. "I don't know if I should let you read these or not, Sergeant. They might make you swell up with pride. He had a lot of wonderful things to say about his squad leader."

The sunlight filtered through the window to Willie's left. It highlighted his face so that the lines of age became more evident. His eyes half closed, and his lips moved for a moment silently. Then he brightened up and said, "I remember your Dad got ahold of some eggs somewhere. Probably stole them from a farmhouse. It was on the day before I got punctured. There were six of us there and five eggs, so when your dad brought them back, there was some argument on how to divide them up. Everyone wanted an egg that day. We were starving, just about. Nothing but K rations for two or three days."

"How did you do it, Dad?"

"Well, Billy Bob Watkins laughed at us and told us the answer. 'Just scramble 'em,' Billy Bob said. So that's what we did. It's been a long time, but I still remember how good those eggs tasted. I don't know where he got it, but Lonnie Shoulders had some hot sauce, a little bottle of it. He just about baptized his. I tried a little of it and near about burned my tongue off. Chief always did like hot stuff like that."

"We're off to see Pete Maxwell's family in a few days, Dad. Charlene's got an open date." He grinned and said, "Pretty nice to have a private plane just to chauffeur me around. Makes me feel important."

Willie put his eyes on Charlene and said, "This young whippersnapper behaving himself?"

"Pretty well, Willie. Why? Did you think he wouldn't?"

"No. I knew he would. He's a good boy. Always has been."

"I don't know about that," Ben said quickly. "I can remember a few times you didn't seem to think so."

"You were just a boy, and you missed out on a lot. I don't know if he told you, Charlene, but I was in pretty bad shape a lot of the time, and Ben had to take over at the newsstand. He missed out on stuff like playing ball and going on camping trips with the Scouts. I never have forgiven myself for that."

"Don't think about it, Dad."

Charlene said quickly, "I wish you would use your parental authority to make this son of yours do something."

"What's that, Doctor?"

"I'd like to read the story he's writing. I know it's not finished yet, but he won't show me a word of it."

"I don't let anybody see my work until it's perfected."

"Oh, you're a prima donna, are you?" Charlene made a face. "I hate you artistic types."

"Well, you scientific types are no better. You don't understand the imaginative spirit."

The two stayed for more than an hour, and there was a great deal of laughter in the room. Mabelene Williams, the black nurse, came down once and said, "You folks makin' a lot of noise. You gonna disturb the other patients."

"It's all right, Mabelene," Willie grinned. "This lady's a doctor. She's giving me treatments."

Mabelene looked doubtfully at Charlene. "Is that right? You're a doctor?"

"That's right, but I wouldn't do much good here. I'm a pediatric surgeon."

"Is that right! Well, I guess it's all right if you wanna make a little noise. You feelin' all right today, Sergeant?"

"Feelin' real good, Mabelene. By the way, where'd you get that name of yours? I never heard it before I met you."

"My mama named me after some eye shadow. I do think it's pretty."

"It is a nice name," Charlene said quickly. "And I've never known anybody named Mabelene before either."

"I'm one of a kind," Mabelene grinned and left the room.

"She's a mighty good nurse. Has to put up with a lot out here," Willie said.

"We'll come and see you after we get back from visiting Pete's family."

"He was a good boy, good soldier."

As the pair left, Charlene said, "I like your dad. It must be hard being cooped up in there."

"I wish I could keep him at home, but I'm never there."

"Now don't go off on a guilt trip about that. I know you come to see him as often as you can."

"No, I don't."

Charlene cast a quick glance at Ben but said nothing as they walked toward the car.

• • •

Two days later Ben was sitting in his office when his editor popped in. Sal Victorio stood for a moment watching Ben, who had his chair tipped back and was staring up at the ceiling. "What are you doing?" Sal demanded.

"I'm writing. Can't you see? I'm creating words, making up a story."

"You're asleep is what you are. How's that story on Christmas coming?"

"Fantastic. Going to be the best editorial on Christmas ever written."

Sal stared at his star reporter then grunted and left.

Ben opened his eyes and leaned forward and put his hand flat on the desk. He had been lonely for the past two days, and the story had not gone well. He slowly reached over, picked up the phone, and dialed a number. He asked for Dr. Delaughter, and by some miracle he got her. "What are you doing?" he said.

"I'm working. What are you doing?"

"Killing time. Not writing a story."

"You have writer's block?"

"There's no such thing."

"There's no such thing as writer's block? I thought there was."

"Did you ever hear of a plumber's block? Did you ever hear a plumber say, 'Oh, I can't unstop that sink. I just don't *feel* it!' Did you ever hear of dishwashing block? No. There are no blocks. Just lazy people. I guess that's what I am."

"Well, I've got the cure for it. I've got a chore for you. I was going to call you."

"For me? You want me to hand you the scalpel while you do the operating?"

"No, thanks." Charlene's voice sounded amused. "I'm going to the children's ward at six o'clock tonight. I want you to go with me."

"Sure. Be glad to."

"And play Santa Claus."

Ben reared back. "Play Santa Claus! No way!"

"You've got to do it. I've got to have a Santa Claus to pass out the gifts."

"I'll pass out the gifts, but I'm not putting on a red suit and stuffing a pillow in."

"Yes, you are. You're bored, and I've got a job for you. Come on, Ben."

"Charlene, Santa Claus is everything I've hated about Christmas."

"Pretty please."

"No! Don't ask me. Good-bye!"

Ben hung up and stared at the phone, then got up and walked across the room to stare out the window. He looked down at the people scurrying around, and as he did, something seemed to turn over within him. He stood there for a long moment struggling then finally shrugged. "It's not as bad as getting stuck in the eye with a sharp stick," he muttered. Going back, he picked up the phone and managed to get Dr. Delaughter again.

"All right. Ho, ho, ho. I'll be Santa Claus. Where do you want me to meet you?"

• • •

"Why, Santa, you look so nice."

Charlene was waiting outside the restroom where Ben had gone to put on his Santa costume. He stood there in the red suit with the black boots, the phony beard that didn't fit and the cap that kept slipping off.

"I feel like an utter fool," he muttered.

"You're a fine Santa Claus. Now, come along. I'll go in and give you an introduction, then you come sweeping in. Let me hear you say ho, ho, ho."

"Ho, ho, ho."

"That's terrible! Give it all you've got. A big ho, ho, ho!"

"Ho, ho, ho!" Ben bellowed. "How's that?"

"Well, it's loud." Charlene laughed. "Come along. You're going to love it."

Charlene pushed a large laundry cart filled with gaily wrapped packages. Ben followed her down the hall, and he turned into a set of double doors, heeding her warning to wait until he heard his cue. "Break a leg, Santa." She punched him in the padding on his stomach, then entered the ward.

Ben stood there listening as she greeted the children. She sounded happy and cheerful, and then he heard her say, "And we have a special visitor tonight who's come all the way from the North Pole. I know it's not Christmas, but Santa couldn't wait to come and see you. Come in, Santa!"

Ben shoved through the doors, glanced around at the beds that lined the wall, and then bellowed, "Ho! ho! ho! Merry Christmas!"

The children returned his greeting. Ben looked around and saw the thin bodies, some of them bandaged, all of them watching him. "Well, it's mighty cold out there, but I just couldn't wait to get here and see you kids."

He went to the first bed and said, "Dr. Delaughter here is going to help me. She's not as pretty as some of the elves that I have making toys up at the North Pole, but she'll have to do. Give me the present for this fine young lady, Doctor." He took the present and held it in one hand. "What's your name, sweetheart?"

"Flora Belle."

The little girl was black and nothing but skin and bones. Her thin face made her eyes look enormous. "Well, Flora Belle, Merry Christmas."

"Thank you, Santa." Flora Belle took the package and said, "Do I have to wait 'til Christmas?"

"No, tonight's Christmas here. Open it right now."

Flora Belle tore the wrapping off and looked up with a shy smile. "It's just what I wanted. A Barbie doll just like me."

"Santa always knows, Flora Belle. What are you going to name her?"

"I'm going to name her Charlene."

"That's a good name, honey. You stick with it."

For the next hour Ben and Charlene went from bed to bed. Charlene had brought more than enough presents, so they made two complete rounds. Finally Charlene said, "All right, now, that's all the presents, but I'm going to tell you a story. Everyone keep your wrapping paper quiet and look at me. It's the best story you've ever heard. It began one night a long time ago when a man and a woman came looking for a room at an inn."

"I know this story," Flora Belle said. "It's about Jesus."

"That's right, Flora Belle. It's about Jesus."

Ben listened as Charlene quoted the Christmas story from Luke word for word, pausing to give it special dramatic touches. Finally, when she was through with the story, the ward was very quiet.

"And now I want you all to remember," Charlene said, "Jesus was born into this world just like you were. He came here because He loved you. Right now you're sick, but He's your best friend. I want you all to remember that no matter how bad you feel, Jesus is with you."

Ben bowed his head as she began to pray, but as she prayed he lifted his eyes and looked around the room. These broken bodies and some broken spirits had been cheered for a moment. Being Santa wasn't so bad after all.

• • •

"Come on. We're going to eat."

"You've got an Italian restaurant lined up?"

"No. I've got my apartment lined up. I'm a good doctor, but I should have been a cook. I'm much better at it."

Ben laughed. "I'll remember that when I want to put you down."

The two went to Charlene's apartment, where she grilled two steaks and baked potatoes while Ben fixed a salad. They sat down and Charlene said, "Do you want to ask the blessing, Ben?"

Ben was silent for a moment then he shook his head. "I'm in no condition to do that."

"Then I'll do it. Lord, we thank You for this food. We thank You for the time we had with the children. Bless every one of them and bless Ben that he might open his eyes to see Jesus. Amen."

Ben looked up and smiled. "You never give up, do you, Doc?"

"I never do. Neither does God. Now buck into that steak."

The two ate, and afterward he helped with the dishes, such as they were.

"Now, you want to see *It's a Wonderful Life*?"

"That thing keeps cropping up! It's an American icon."

"It gives people hope, I think. Nothing wrong with having hope, but I won't make you watch it again."

The two of them sat on the couch and talked for a long time. Ben found himself telling Charlene things that he had never told anyone. Finally he glanced at his watch and started. "It's nearly eleven thirty!"

"My, how time goes by when you're having fun," Charlene said.

"I'll get out of your way." Ben rose. She got his coat, he put it on, then he turned to face her. She was looking at him strangely, and a silence came between them. They felt something warm but unsettling lay between them. Ben saw in the woman that stood before him an emotion that strongly worked and left its fugitive impression on her face. But he thought the urges of a lone man, perhaps, always moved like a compass to a certain woman, and this woman was like none that he had ever known. She held his glance as direct as his own, and he could not hide the desire that was in him. She was near enough to be touched, and he wanted to touch her, for her nearness sharpened all his long-felt hungers. She was, he recognized, a woman with fire and spirit and yet with a soft depth. He wondered if she revealed these things on purpose or if he dreamed them. She smiled, her expression frank then soft. There was a sweetness in her, and Ben Raines realized that no other woman had stirred him as this one. For one instant they were close to something, but then suddenly she put out her hand and he took it.

"You did a good thing tonight, Ben, an unselfish thing. I knew you would hate being Santa Claus, but it was good."

"It wasn't bad. As a matter of fact, it was good for me. Good night."

Ben left then quickly, and as he walked toward his car, the stars above were cold and glittering. He looked up and they seemed somehow lonely, which was strange. Suddenly he realized that he was the one who was lonely, and the loneliness closed about him as he got into his car and drove away.

Chapter
EIGHT
ॐ

L os Angeles spread out beneath them, and Ben remarked, "Look at the smog. I think you could walk on it."

"I'd rather not try."

"Is it always this busy?"

"This is Orange County Airport," Charlene said. "Used to be called John Wayne Airport. Be glad we're not going into Los Angeles International Airport. That one really *is* crowded."

Charlene brought the plane in for a perfect landing. As she taxied toward the hanger, she turned to smile at Ben. "You're getting a little more comfortable. Are you learning to trust my flying a bit more?"

"I think I am. You're a wonderful pilot, Charlene."

Charlene taxied the plane up to the hangar and shut the engine off. The two got out, and Ben stood over to one side while she made the usual arrangements for having the plane refueled and rechecked. When she came over to him, he said, "Let's don't rent a car. I've heard about Los Angeles traffic."

"Yes, a cab would be better."

They took no luggage, for their plan was to visit Pete

94

Maxwell, then fly home that night. "Lots warmer here than in Chicago," Ben remarked.

"Yes. I thought about moving to California just for the weather, but then someone told me that everything loose rolls to California so I decided not to."

A row of cabs in front of the airport awaited them, and when they got into the first in line, a battered Crown Victoria, Ben gave the address to the driver, a small dark-skinned man. "We'd like to go to 1230 Maple Avenue."

"Yes."

The driver pulled out, and Ben saw that Charlene was trying to raise the window on her side. The cold wind was blowing her hair. "The window won't go up," Ben said.

"Is broken."

"It's pretty cold back here. Would you turn the heater up, please?"

"No heater. Is out of order."

Ben glared at the man and was on the verge of telling him they'd get a cab with working windows and heaters, but when he glanced at Charlene he saw that she was grinning at him. "What?" he demanded.

"Tribulation worketh patience," she said.

"I don't want patience; I want to get warm."

"Think about your ancestors," Charlene said. "They didn't even have windows in the Mayflower. And no heaters, either."

Ben suddenly laughed. "The Raines folk missed that boat. I think they came over on a cattle boat or something."

"Cattle boats don't have heaters either."

Ben threw up his hands in a gesture of defeat. "OK, you win."

Charlene studied the traffic as the driver changed lanes with absolutely no use of the turn signals. "Don't you ever signal, driver?"

"Is not working."

"Figures," Ben laughed. He settled back and looked out the window. "I don't know much about Pete Maxwell. Dad told me his wife passed away and that he was living with his daughter and her husband."

"He's retired, I suppose."

"Oh, yes. Worked for the sanitation department."

"The unsung heroes."

"What?"

Charlene smiled at him. "The workers of the sanitation department went on strike in Evanston three years ago. It was frightful! The garbage piled up like mountains in the streets. The smell would knock you down."

"That happened in Chicago too. You never think about things like that until they happen,

"Maybe you could write a story—'The Unsung Heroes of Chicago.'"

"Maybe I could." Ben suddenly laughed. "The sanitation workers are a lot more noble than the politicians in Chicago."

The two ignored the cold blasts of air, and finally the cab pulled up in front of a house and the cabbie said, "Twelve dollars and thirty cents." He didn't bother to get out but reached back and took the money that Ben extended. "Keep the change."

"Want me to wait?"

"No. Don't think so."

"Here's my card. Give me a call if you need to go back to the airport."

"All right. We'll do that."

The two of them walked toward the house, and Ben said, "I should have called before we came."

"Why didn't you?"

"Because I'm a careless, slovenly person. I did call last week, and Mrs. Taylor said to come anytime."

"That's his daughter?"

"Yes. Hope he's here."

Ben rang the doorbell, and almost at once it opened and a middle-aged woman greeted them. "Yes?"

"Mrs. Taylor?"

"Yes, I am."

"I'm Ben Raines, and this is Dr. Delaughter. I called last week about your father."

"Oh, yes," Mrs. Taylor said. "Come in, both of you." As soon as the two were inside, she said "Dad isn't home right now. He goes to the nursing home every Tuesday and Saturday."

"I should have called."

Mrs. Taylor said, "If you'd like to wait here, that would be fine—or maybe you'd like to catch him at Fair Haven."

"Is it far?"

"Not at all—no more than ten blocks. I'll be glad to take you."

"Oh, we can walk if you'll give us directions." The two listened as Mrs. Taylor gave them directions. "You can't miss it. Dad has his car, so after he's finished there, why don't you come and have dinner with us."

"Oh, that would be an imposition," Ben protested.

"Dad's been looking forward to visiting with you. He stays busy at the nursing home, but if you come here, there'll be plenty of time to talk."

Neither Ben nor Charlene were inclined to accept the invitation, but Mrs. Taylor insisted so strongly that they agreed. "Dinner will be ready by the time you get back," she said firmly, and practically shoved them out the door.

"I guess we've got a free meal at least," Ben said. "I hate to barge in."

"So do I, but it's a good chance to speak with him. Come on, race you to the nursing home!" She started off at a brisk pace, and Ben had to hurry to keep up with her.

By the time they reached the nursing home, Ben was panting. "I miss that beautiful cab!" he gasped.

"You need fresh air and exercise," Charlene grinned. She was not even breathing hard, and said, "We'll double-time it back to the house."

The nursing home was a two-story building of red brick. The lawn in front was carefully manicured, but the building itself was old. As they walked inside, Charlene noted that there was a feeling of age about it. "I guess all nursing homes smell alike," she said as they approached the desk.

"We're looking for Peter Maxwell," Ben said to the woman behind the desk.

"You'll have to run him down." The speaker was a powerfully built woman with dyed red hair and far too much makeup. "Pete's hard to catch. He goes from one room to another. You'll just have to hunt for him."

Ben hesitated. "We don't actually know him."

The nurse laughed. "You'll know Pete when you see him."

"How will we do that?" Charlene asked.

"Because he's the only person you'll see wearing a clown outfit."

"How's that?" Ben asked, confused by the description.

"Pete likes to dress up in different rigs for his visits here. It'd make a dog laugh to see what he comes up with. Last week he got a Charlie Chaplin outfit. Looked just like Chaplin—cane, little moustache, and all!"

"What other outfits has he worn?"

"Law, I can't tell you! Once he came as a sailor—and one time he dressed up like a fat woman!" The nurse laughed out loud. "He was a sight that day!"

"Has he been doing this a long time?" Charlene asked.

"For years! I've worked here for twelve years, and he'd been coming a long time before I got here." The nurse nodded and said, "The patients all look forward to his visits like he was the president. He knows them every one—better than some of the help, I'd have to say."

"Well, I guess we can find a clown," Ben smiled. "Thanks, Nurse."

"You're welcome."

The two walked on down the hallway, and, as always, it gave Ben a feeling of depression. But then he heard the sound of laughter coming from a room, and he said, "My guess is that's Pete."

The two of them came to an open door and saw Pete Maxwell, looking for all the world like a Ringling Brothers clown, juggling three balls. Two extremely aged men were watching. They stood there as Maxwell told jokes and juggled, then when he turned and saw them, Ben said quickly, "Mr. Maxwell?"

He nodded and said, "That's me. I'm Pete. Who are you?"

Ben walked in and said, "I'm Ben Raines, and this is Dr. Charlene Delaughter."

Maxwell was somewhere in his late seventies, Ben guessed, but his eyes were bright. "I know you, do I?"

"You were in my dad's squad in the war. He was—"

"Raines! Why, Willie Raines! You're his son, I take it."

"Yes, I am. Maxwell's thin face lit up. He put out his hand, and when Ben took it he found that the old man's bones were fragile as the bones of a bird. "Willie Raines. I hear from Willie pretty often. He calls me on my birthday. How is Willie? He's OK, ain't he?"

"Yes. He's fine."

"Well, let's go get something to drink."

"Oh, I'm not thirsty," Ben protested.

"I am. Clowning is hard work. Come on, the kitchen is down here."

Maxwell led them to the kitchen, where he greeted two workers with smiles and they quickly provided soft drinks for Maxwell and his guests. Maxwell led them toward the tables and waved toward a chair and said, "You take that one, Doctor." He got them seated, then said, "I've been looking forward to your visit. Now, tell me about this story you're going to write."

Pete listened as Ben explained the idea of the story, and when he had finished, Pete exclaimed, "You know, that's a great idea. I'm glad I thought of it!" He laughed at Ben's expression. "I always thought somebody would have done something like that. Willie's awful proud of you. Talks about you all the time in his letters."

Ben had gotten his notebook out and said, "I would like to hear your side of the story about the action at Bastogne. Your sister has invited us to dinner, so we can talk there, but I'd like to hear about it from your point of view."

"Well, it wasn't no picnic," Pete shrugged. "We knew it wouldn't be. We just got out of Market Garden and that was bad enough, and then fightin' around hedgerows all over France. By the time we got to Bastogne we was whittled down. Wasn't but six of us left, but I guess you know all that."

"Yes. Charlene's dad was one of the squad."

"Delaughter! Why, sure. Charlie Delaughter. A fine fellow! How is he?"

"Dad passed away a few years ago, Pete."

"Oh, sorry to hear that. He was a good guy. Always up, no matter how bad things were. The rest of us would gripe and complain, but old Charlie always found something good to say. Say you're a doctor?"

"A baby doctor."

"Well, that's fine. The world needs more baby doctors."

Ben took lots of notes, for Pete liked to talk. His eyes were the liveliest thing about him, and he seemed to be tiring.

Finally Ben said, "Well, we don't want to wear you out, Pete. We'll be going."

"Nothin' doin'. You're just in time to help with the Bible study. What time is it?"

Ben looked at his watch. "It's four o'clock."

"Just right. They'll be waitin' down in the rec room. Some of them will be watchin' soap operas or game shows, but we have our Bible study every Tuesday afternoon at four o'clock. They'll either have to sit and listen or go. Either of you two play a pianer?"

"I play a little," Charlene said. "It's been a long time."

"You know any hymns?"

"Yes. That's about all I do know."

"Good. You'll play the pianer, and Ben, you're the tune heister."

"Wait a minute," Ben said, "I'm no singer."

"Come on now, Ben." A smile brightened Pete Maxwell's face. "Your dad, he never backed out of nothin' that I ever found out about. How about it?"

Ben glanced at Charlene and saw she was waiting to hear his answer. He hesitated only a moment and shrugged. "Well, I probably don't remember most of the songs, but I'll do the best I can."

"Now you're talkin'! Come on, let's get this show on the road!" Pete was talking all the time. "You know, I've been thinking about organizing the Bed Pan Olympics around here. What do you think?"

He kept them entertained all the way down the hall and around the corner. When they entered a large room, they found a small group there. The television was blaring, but Pete called out, "Hey, Bertha, turn that sin box off. It's time to study the Word of God. We're gonna have a holy hootenanny today!"

All of the members of the Bible study were elderly, of course. Two or three of them looked like they were completely out of it, but Pete went at it as if he were addressing ninety thousand people in a coliseum. "We got some guests today. Sister Charlene here is going to play the piano, and Brother Ben, he's gonna do the singing. OK, brother and sister, let it rip!"

Charlene went over to the old upright, made a face as she ran her fingers over the keys, for it was sadly out of tune. Nevertheless, she began playing "The Old Rugged Cross." Ben found himself able to get through that one. They were using tattered paperback hymn books called *Heavenly Highways* that looked like they had come over on the ark. As Ben lead the singing as best he could, he was thinking about his early days when his parents had taken him to the little church every Sunday. He had not thought about that in a long time, but now he could see himself as a youngster sitting between his parents, sometimes listening to the preaching, sometimes filling in the round letters, such as *e*'s and *o*'s, in the hymnbook with a pencil.

They struggled through the service, and Ben discovered that Charlene had a fine soprano voice. He himself had a fairly good voice, and then Pete insisted they sing a duet together, "On Christ the Solid Rock I Stand, All Other Ground Is Sinking Sand."

He whispered to Charlene, "I remember my folks used to sing that song together. Mom played the piano."

After the song service was over, Pete took over and asked for testimonies. Several of the patients managed to say a few words. One of them, a woman who looked to be in her nineties, said, "I'm closer to home than I ever was. Glory to God! I'll be there soon. Bless the name of Jesus."

All the other testimonies were that simple, but finally Pete said, "Now, you visitors, let's hear your story about how you found Jesus."

Charlene cast a quick look at Ben and saw that he was speechless. Immediately she began telling how she was converted. It was a simple testimony. She had been saved when she was fourteen years old, and she ended by saying, "I was headed down the wrong road, but when I found the Lord Jesus, things went right."

Pete was busy throwing in amens, and, finally, when Charlene finished, he said, "I can't give this fella's testimony, but I can give his dad's." He went on to tell the story about how Sergeant Willie Raines had saved his whole squad, what was left of it, at Bastogne. "This fella right here, his dad saved every one of us that Christmas. He always said," Pete reminisced, "that there was an angel there that kept him and told him what to do, and I believe him." He turned and said quietly, "I know you're proud of your dad, Ben."

And suddenly Ben spoke up. "Yes, I am proud of him. I haven't always honored him as I should, but I found out that he did a brave thing and gave life to some good people."

• • •

After the service was over the director of the nursing home, who had come to stand with his back against the wall, came over to thank them. "I'm Tom Jennings," he said, "the director here. I want to thank you folks for comin' by."

"I'm glad we could do it."

"I heard what Pete said about your father. Those men saved our country. I'd like to shake his hand, but since I can't I'll just shake yours."

"Is Pete always like this?" Charlene asked the director.

"I call him the apostle of the hopeless. He's in bad shape, Miss. He's in pain right now, but you'd never know it. We get a lot of sad people in here, and Pete feels it's his calling to go around and preach to them and cheer them up. This wouldn't be the same place without him!"

• • •

The dinner with the Taylors was excellent. Pearl Taylor was a fine cook, and her husband Thad was a smiling man who showed his obvious affection for his father-in-law.

After the meal, they adjourned to the family room where Ben got the whole story of his father's heroism from one who was there. He got it all on tape, and when it was time to go, he said, "I'll play this for Dad. It'll mean a lot to him—as it does to me."

"Be sure you send me a copy of that story of yours, Ben," Pete insisted. "And tell Willie I'll be seein' him soon." He saw that the words startled Ben and said, "I don't mean here. I mean the old squad's going to be together again one of these days. Tell Willie I'll meet him on the other side."

"I'll tell him, Pete," Ben said. He stepped back as Charlene said good-bye to the old man. They thanked the Taylors, promising to keep in touch, then went out to the cab that Mr. Taylor had called for them.

Neither of them said much on the way to the airport, each occupied with private thoughts. The quiet continued as they went through the takeoff procedures, but when they were seated in the plane just before takeoff, Ben looked over and saw that Charlene was crying. "It was sad, wasn't it?"

"Sad and yet not sad," Charlene said. "Pete's so brave. How hard it must be to keep going."

"A garbage man," Ben whispered, "but his life has meant more than mine!"

Suddenly it all caught up with Ben, and he felt his eyes mist over. He blinked them rapidly and bit his lip, but despite himself tears formed. He felt them running down his cheeks, and then he heard Charlene say, "It's all right to cry, Ben." He felt a hand on his cheek and turned his head away. His throat was so thick he couldn't answer. He had seen royal courage this day, a courage that he knew he himself did not have. He sat quietly in the seat as Charlene took the plane off the ground, and then they headed back to Chicago. They had been flying twenty minutes when he took out his handkerchief, blew his nose and said, "I haven't cried since I was twelve years old."

"I have," Charlene said. "Men like Pete Maxwell, they make you want to cry." She held the plane steady, then she whispered, "But they make you want to shout, too!"

Chapter
NINE

For a full four days after the flight to Los Angeles Ben had felt strange. He could not get the thought of the survivors of Bastogne out of his mind. He went every day to see his father, and as he went in on Thursday, Mabelene Williams smiled at him in a way that was not customary. "Well, you're back again. Gettin' to be a regular habit."

"I guess so, Mabelene."

"I didn't know you had a heart." She grinned broadly and rolled her eyes. "I thought you was like that scarecrow in the *Wizard of Oz*. You remember him? He didn't have no heart— but after the wizard gave him one, he done real fine!"

"I remember, but it doesn't work that way in real life. I'm not surprised you'd feel that way. I was a pretty bad son for a long time."

Mabelene was staring at him thoughtfully. "What got into you? Have you hit the Glory Road?"

"What?"

"You got yourself saved? You been baptized in the blood of the Lamb? Are you born again?"

Ben could not help smiling. "I guess not, Mabelene."

"Well, you gonna be. I'll have my whole church prayin' for you."

"Which church you go to?"

"The Fire-baptized Two-seed-in-the-Spirit Predestination Baptist!"

Ben grinned. "Sounds like a good one to me."

"You come visit with us sometime. You'll see what it's like when the Lord moves. But I'm happy you come and seein' Mr. Willie. He's a good man, and I think you are, too, if you'd just let yourself be."

Ben went in to see his father, who was sitting at the small table reading the Bible. He put it aside and said, "Hello, Son. How's the story going?"

"Pretty good, Dad. Have you heard from Pete?"

"Sure did. Got a letter today. He said you and Charlene stirred the place up out there. Said she played the piano and you did the singin', and it was like an old time revival."

"Well, you know my singing wasn't that good. Charlene's a good piano player though."

"That woman is something," Willie said. "Flies an airplane. Plays a piano. Does surgery."

"She's a good cook, too."

"Well, how about that checker game? I'm ready to beat you again."

"Again!" Ben grinned. "You haven't beat me in a week."

"I'm about to begin to commence to start," Willie said. "Sit down."

Willie always played checkers with enthusiasm. When he jumped a man, he slammed it down so that the other men were likely to be bounced off the board. When Ben took a man, Willie groaned and carried on as if he had lost a wisdom tooth.

Finally, after the second game, Willie said, "That's enough for now." He sat back in his chair, and Ben went to get something to drink. His dad liked root beer, and fortunately they had it in the drink machine. "Two beers coming up," he said. He set the bottles down, twisted the caps off and said, "Tell me some more about when you were in the army, Dad."

"Why, I done told you all of it."

"No, you haven't. How about the training?"

Ben sat back and listened while his father talked. He knew his father was making it sound easier than it really was, and he thought as he sat there, *How I have misjudged my dad. All my life I put him down and didn't have sense enough to see what a real man he was.*

"What about that woman doctor Charlene?"

Ben was thinking of other things, and he blinked with surprise. "What do you mean? She's a doctor."

"I know that. I mean I *like* that woman. How do *you* feel about her?"

Ben did not know how to answer. In all truth he had thought about Charlene Delaughter a great deal, but now he said, "Well, she's a good doctor, a good pilot, and a good cook."

"You talk like a sophomore in high school. What I'm asking you, Son, is how do you *feel* about her?"

"I know what you're asking, Dad, but nothing would ever come of it. She wouldn't be interested in a second-rate writer like me."

Willie smiled slowly. He leaned forward and tapped Ben's hand with his fingertip. "Don't be too sure about that. Your mother, she was interested in a second-rate guy like me."

Ben could not answer that, so he changed the subject. "We'll be making another trip as soon as Charlene can get away. We're going to see Billy Bob Watkins."

"They still live in Arkansas?"

"Yeah. A place called Bald Knob. That's a funny name."

"There's lots of funny names in Arkansas—like Toadsuck Ferry."

Ben stared at his father. "You made that up!"

"Did not. There's a Whitewash, Arkansas, too, and a Cotton Plant. Folks knew how to make up names with a little bite in 'em back in those days. I've missed Billy Bob. He was a good soldier. They were all good soldiers in our squad and in our company. You tell Billy Bob what I said about him."

"I'll do that, Dad." He got up and said his good-byes, and then when he got to the door, Willie's voice caught him. "You hang on to that doctor. I think she's a keeper."

. . .

Ben and Charlene had landed at Fayetteville, rented a car, and after a drive through some beautiful country were approaching the farm of Billy Bob Watkins, which was nestled in a fertile valley in the Ozarks. As they drove toward it, Ben said, "In the fall the colors here are fabulous."

"It's beautiful country, Ben."

Ben pulled up in front of the large stone and cedar house and got out of the car. He opened the door for Charlene, and they both looked at the large barns and the open fields populated with cattle such as Charlene had never seen. "What kind of cows are those, Ben?"

"I think they're Black Angus, but I'm no expert."

The two stepped up on the porch and were met by a tall woman in her mid-seventies, Ben guessed. She was large—not fat, just large. She had direct gray eyes and a firm mouth and beautiful silver hair. She greeted them in a soft flat drawl. "You must be Mr. Raines. I'm Lou Dean Watkins."

"This is Dr. Delaughter, Mrs. Watkins. Doctor, this is Billy Bob's wife."

"I'm proud to meet you, Doctor. My husband went huntin' with our grandson, but he'll be back directly. Come on in the house. It's cold out here. You got your Christmas shoppin' all done?"

Lou Dean Watkins fired questions rapidly in her flat Arkansas drawl. And finally after a time, when she had discovered everything she could about the story that Ben was working on, she said, "I'm pleased at what you say about the story."

"Were you and your husband married young, Mrs. Watkins?" Ben asked.

Lou Dean Watkins laughed. "We was sweethearts in the fifth grade. Only reason we didn't start sooner was that my folks didn't move into the valley till then."

"Did you have other boyfriends?" Charlene asked.

"Law, no! First time I seen Billy Bob I knew we was going to get married. He says the same thing."

"I think that's beautiful, Mrs. Watkins," Charlene said. "So many marriages don't last these days."

"Well, we knew ours would."

"Did you ever have arguments?"

Lou Dean Watkins' eyes danced. "I made the preacher put an extra condition in our ceremony."

"What kind of condition?"

"That we'd never go to sleep mad." She laughed aloud and scared a canary in a cage by slapping her hands. "Once we didn't sleep for three days and nights. I guess we both saw that there wasn't nothing for it but to make up—and we did."

"What was Billy Bob like before he was in the army?"

"Just the same as he was after he went in," Lou Dean smiled. "He was always a good boy, a good baseball player, good on the farm. He worked hard, like we all did in those days. I wanted to get married before he went to the war, but he made me wait."

"He was a fine soldier, my dad says."

"I want to show you somethin'." Lou Dean Watkins got up and left the room. She came back with a small flat box in her hand. "We're all mighty proud of this in our family. Billy Bob won't never let it be mentioned, but he's not here." She opened the box and handed it to Ben. He took it, and his eyes opened wide. "Why, this is the Congressional Medal of Honor!"

"That's what it is. They say it's the highest medal a soldier can get in this country."

"It is," Charlene said. "I've never even seen one." She took the box and ran her fingers over the medal. "What did he do, Mrs. Watkins?"

"It was along like what your dad done, Mr. Raines. Wait a minute. I just thought of somethin'. You sit right there." Once again Lou Dean left the room. She came back with some letters and sorted through them. "This is the one right here. It's about your dad." She opened it and read:

"I'd be dead if it wasn't for Willie Raines. He was the best soldier I ever saw. I got my mind made up. If I ever get in a tough spot, I will remember Willie and try to do what he did."

She handed the letter to Ben, who took it and read the words for himself. "I'd like to have a copy of this, Mrs. Watkins."

"You go right ahead. Take it down to the post office and make a copy of all of 'em. Your dad's in several of them."

"I'll do that, if you don't mind."

"Well, about what Billy done. His squad got pinned down, and there was some men out there that was shot. They was out in the open, and they couldn't get back. They was all wounded, don't you see. So, Billy, he ran out and got one of 'em. He got shot, but he got him back anyhow." Lou Dean Watkins' voice trembled then, and she had to bite her lip. "He brought in five men, one at a time. Got wounded twice more, but he kept on until he got 'em all out. He almost died gettin' the last one out."

"What a wonderful thing!" Charlene whispered.

"He was such a good boy. He was a Christian, too. He got saved in a revival meeting the summer he went to war. He talked about that a lot, how that if he got kilt, he'd be with Jesus." Suddenly she lifted her head and rose to go to the window. "There they come now. Looks like they got a mess of squirrels."

Both Ben and Charlene got to their feet, their eyes fixed on the door. Two men stepped inside, both tall and lanky. They both had light blue eyes and tow-colored hair. "This is my husband, and this is our grandson Robert Lee. This is Mr. Raines, Billy, and Dr. Delaughter."

Billy Bob's eyes crinkled as he smiled and came forward putting out his hand. "I'm right proud to know you." His hand was rough and clamped down on Ben's like a Stiltson wrench. "You mind me of your daddy. Got the same kind of look around your eyes Willie had."

"Dr. Delaughter is the daughter of Charlie Delaughter."

Billy Bob's eyes opened wide, and he put his hand out and took Charlene's. "I swan! You're Charlie's girl? Well ain't that fine! Me and Charlie had some good times."

"He mentioned you so often in his letters. I'll make copies and send them to you."

"'Preciate that, I purely would!"

The younger man stepped forward and shook hands with Ben. His grip was just as powerful, and he said, "I've heard about your dad since the day I was born, Mr. Raines. Every time I act up, Pop says, 'Willie Raines wouldn't have done a thing like that! Why don't you act like him?'"

"That's a good way to make a boy hate someone," Ben smiled. He liked the looks of the young man, and asked, "Are you in college?"

"Yes, sir, I'm a sophomore at the University of Arkansas."

"A Razorback, are you?" Charlene smiled. "I always root for the Razorbacks."

"Why, are you from Arkansas, Doctor?" Robert Lee asked.

"No, I'm a Yankee, but my husband was born and reared in Little Rock. He played for the Razorbacks."

"Ain't that a caution now!" Billy Bob exclaimed. "Robert Lee here, he's the quarterback for the Hogs."

"Just a back-up quarterback, Pop," the young man protested.

"Well, I wrote a letter to the coach tellin' him he was makin' a big mistake not using you."

"Pop! You didn't!"

"Shore I did." Billy Bob nodded emphatically. "You know that poem I like so much:

> I hate to be a-kickin'
> I always long for peace,
> But the wheel that does the squeakin'
> Is the one that gets the grease.

"I told you not to write that fool letter," Lou Dean shook her head with disapproval. "You are the stubbornest man I ever seen!"

"No, Lou Dean, *you're* stubborn—I'm *firm*."

"Did you get any squirrels?"

"Did I ever not get squirrels? Course I got squirrels! Between us we got fourteen."

"I got ten, and Pop got four," Robert Lee grinned.

"I had something in my eye," Billy Bob said. "Now, you go out there and clean them squirrels. Be sure you save the brains for the doctor here."

Ben caught a glimpse of Charlene's face and laughed outright. "Don't look like that, Dr.. It can't be any worse than eating snails."

"I heard them frogs over the water ate snails," Billy Bob said with disapproval on his bronzed face. "Just shows you how depraved they are. Now, you get to them squirrels, Lee. Ma, you start cooking a bodacious supper."

"And what will you do while Robert Lee and I do the work?" Lou Dean demanded.

"Why somebody around here's got to take care of making talk with our guests, ain't they?" Billy Bob demanded with a hurt look on his face. "Now you folks come on and set down. I want to hear all about your daddy, Ben—and yours too, Doc."

• • •

Ben and Charlene were held prisoners by the Watkins clan. They protested that they couldn't possibly impose on them, but in the end, they spent the night.

"My wife is plumb downright stubborn," Billy Bob whispered loudly. "And when she don't get her way, she pouts for days."

"I do not!"

"Oh, she does," Billy Bob nodded. "I had to build a special room for her. Call it her 'pout room.' She goes in there and won't eat until we all give in to her. Y'all will just have to stay or I might have to divorce her."

"I don't guess you'd put up with that, would you, Mrs. Watkins?"

"Don't pay no attention to his foolishness! He loves to torment me."

"But Ma, you don't know how interesting you be!"

In the end, Ben and Charlene stayed. Charlene sampled squirrel brains mixed in with scrambled eggs. They sat up until nearly dawn, with Billy Bob talking about the squad. He never mentioned his own decorations, but couldn't say enough about the rest of the men he served with.

"They was good men," he said. "No better men ever lived."

"Tell your dad one Razorback is sure grateful," Robert Lee said. "If he hadn't saved Pop's life, I wouldn't be here."

"That's right," Billy Bob said, and a thoughtful look crossed his face. "Your daddy always said an angel told him how to nail that Kraut mortar. You going to put that in your story, Son?"

Ben didn't answer for a moment. He felt Charlene's eyes on him, and finally he said, "'The Angel of Bastogne.' Makes a good title, doesn't it?" He turned to face Charlene and nodded slowly. "Yes, I think Dad would like it if the angel were in the story."

• • •

They left the next morning, promising to keep in touch, and drove back to the regional airport. It wasn't much of an airport, but at least a plane could land. When they got in and took off, Ben talked for some time about how he had changed his mind about the story.

"What do you mean, Ben?"

"Well, I was always a cynical guy. I'd seen that movie so much, *It's a Wonderful Life*, and I didn't believe most of it. I didn't believe things turned out right. I've seen a lost of misery, like all of us have—you more than most, I'd guess. So, I was going to write a story about how most sacrifice is in vain. But I can't say that now."

"No, you can't. It's been wonderful meeting these families, considering how your dad was instrumental in keeping them alive. I think—" Suddenly the plane's engine coughed and then stopped without warning.

"What's wrong?" Ben said in alarm.

"I don't know." Charlene was tense. She was moving her hands over the controls. Ben knew better than to trouble her when she was trying to get the engine back to life.

The plane began to lose altitude, and Charlene said in a terse, tight voice, "We may be going down, Ben."

"You mean crash?"

Charlene did not answer. She was working frantically, but the plane was dropping like a stone. Ben braced his feet against the floorboard and stared at the ground below. It seemed to be rushing up at them at a tremendous rate of speed.

He suddenly recognized how unimportant some things were. He was going to die in a few moments, he was sure of that, and what had he accomplished with his life? He had become nothing but a cynical man afraid to admit that there was good in the world. In a dark world there were lights, and he had fled from them.

Suddenly, when it seemed that the ground was no more than a few hundred feet away, the engine burst into life. Charlene hauled back on the yoke, and the wings bit into the air. They skimmed the top of some trees, and Charlene fought to gain altitude.

"We'll be all right now, Ben," she said, finally expelling her breath. She turned to look at him. "Are you all right?"

"I . . . I thought it was over."

"So did I. Closest call I've ever had in a plane. It shook me up. You think you're ready for things like this, but I guess you never are."

Ben said nothing. He was pale and took out a handkerchief to wipe the perspiration from his face. Charlene talked about what the possibilities might be and said, "I'm putting down at the next airfield. We'll have it checked over."

"All right."

They landed twenty minutes later with the engine running perfectly. When she shut it off and turned to Ben, she said, "I'm sorry. I know that was frightening for you."

"It made me think a little bit. No, it made me think a lot."

"What did you think, Ben?"

"I thought how worthless my life has been and how selfish and how—I'd like to do better."

"Would you really, Ben?"

"Yes, but I'm afraid."

"You don't have to be afraid. All God wants is 'I want to.' If you want to, Ben, you can have a good life. You can have Jesus Christ, and that's the best life there is."

Charlene always carried a little Testament with her, and she shared verses with Ben for a few moments. Then she said, "It's not hard to be saved. It's hard to live the Christian life, but to come into the kingdom of God, it's what God wants for you. All you have to do is turn and call."

"Turn from what?"

"*From* everything that you know displeases God and turn *to* what the Bible says: 'Whosoever shall call upon the name of the Lord shall be saved.' I've been praying for you, Ben, and I'm going to pray right now. And while I'm praying, within your own heart I wish you'd call on Jesus and ask Him to save you."

Charlene began praying, and Ben felt that he had not enough strength to even lift his hand. He bowed his head, and he felt tremors go through his whole body. But suddenly he knew that Charlene was right. He had seen enough of his father and mother to know that there was such a thing as a real Christian. He had seen Charlene. He had seen Pete Maxwell. He had seen enough. He began trying to pray in his heart, and finally as he did, tears began to roll down his cheeks. He spoke aloud and asked God to come into his heart. Finally he was aware that Charlene was quiet. He lifted his head and wiped his face with his handkerchief.

"I know you called on God that time," Charlene said quietly.

"I did, and from this moment on I'm following Jesus Christ and letting him direct me every day."

Charlene reached out and took his hand and held it. Her eyes were glistening. "I'm so happy for you, Ben. And think how happy your dad will be!"

Chapter
TEN
~

B en sat at his writing table, the pale sunlight streaming in
through the windows. The beams caught the myriad of
dust particles as in a yellow spotlight. The motes were stirred
up mostly by Clara Munson, who vigorously pushed the
vacuum cleaner over the carpet. For Clara the war against
dirt was a personal thing, and she scowled at the carpet as if
it were a flesh-and-blood enemy. From time to time she would
call a truce with the dirt and cast a furtive glance toward her
employer. Clara visualized herself as a psychologist, although
she would not have called it that. It was her firm conviction
that she understood people—not what was on the outside but
what was on the inside. For three years now she had studied
Benjamin Raines, and up until recently she was certain that
she had him firmly classified.

Clara's face turned itself into a frown, and finally she
reached down and turned the vacuum cleaner off. As soon as
the roar stopped, she could hear the song that Benjamin was
singing. It was a Christmas carol and one she knew well, "Joy
to the World, The Lord Has Come."

Clara moved around until she could see Ben Raines' face more clearly. The puzzlement that had begun to trouble her showed itself more plainly. *He ain't never sung no Christmas songs before. Not since I been here anyway,* she thought belligerently. She saw he was smiling as his fingers moved over the computer keyboard, and he was swaying from side to side in tune to his own music.

Finally Clara could stand it no longer. "I don't know what's got into you. I never knew you to sing no Christmas song before."

Ben grinned at his cleaning lady. It amused him to cause her to wonder about his behavior. He leaned back, locked his hands behind his head and arched his body, for he had been hunched over the computer a long time. He stretched, extending his arms, then nodded. "I've decided to participate in Christmas this year, Clara. I'm even going to give you a Christmas present. What would you like?"

Clara Munson stared at her employer. She did not like for people to step outside the mold that she created for them in her mind. Still, there was something pleasant about the way Ben Raines looked. "All you ever gave me before was a ten-dollar bill in a card."

"I know. So this time I'm going to give you a present nice enough to make up for all the years I've missed."

Clara was speechless. She knew very well that Ben Raines did not believe in Christmas or in very much of anything else. Still, as she tried to think of a remark that would put him in his place, nothing came to mind. Finally she sniffed, "Well, I suppose people can change."

"They certainly can, Clara."

"What made you change?"

Ben was tempted to launch into the story, but knew that he would have to give up working, for Clara would have to know every detail. She had a curiosity as long as a piece of rope, so he simply smiled at her and said, "I just discovered that I'd been missing a lot, so you think about that present." He hit the save button on his computer, got to his feet, and said, "I've got to go down to the office."

"You want me to come in Christmas Day?"

"Come in on Christmas Day! I should say not! The very idea." Ben walked over and suddenly put one arm around Clara and squeezed her. "That's no way to spend Christmas, and right now I wish you a Merry Christmas, Clara." He laughed for no reason, then plucked his coat off the coat rack and slipped it over his shoulders. "Merry Christmas! Ho! Ho! Ho!" He stepped outside, and Clara stood staring at the door he had closed behind him. She tried to think of some explanation for all this, and finally she said, "He don't seem like he's taken to drinkin'. I wonder if men go through a change of life like women do."

She pondered that for a moment, then her brow wrinkled up. "Well, we'll see if it lasts. That's what we'll do." She walked over and threw the switch on the vacuum cleaner and began pushing it vigorously back and forth across the carpet.

• • •

Ben locked his car and walked rapidly down the street toward the newspaper office. He passed no fewer than three

Salvation Army red pots hanging from black tripods and all watched over by the Salvation Army folk. Each time he stopped, pulled his billfold out, and extracted a five-dollar bill. The two ladies and the one man that guarded the treasure looked surprised and said with considerable enthusiasm, "Thank you, sir! Merry Christmas to you."

"A Merry Christmas to you," Ben had given back to each.

As he approached the door that housed the newspaper, he encountered Nick Farrell coming out. "Merry Christmas, Nick," he said.

Farrell was a tall, thin man, a sports writer, and he had the stub of a cigar in his mouth. There was talk that he had been born with it in his mouth, for no one ever saw him without it. He chewed on it for a moment then nodded. "You're feeling chipper."

"It's Christmas, Nick."

"It always is this time of year."

"You done all your shopping yet?"

"No. I let my wife take care of all that."

"You shouldn't. You ought to do it yourself. Get into the spirit of Christmas."

"Is this Benjamin Raines I see before me? Is this the guy that every year gripes about the commercialism of Christmas? I think not. It must be Benjamin's body taken over by an alien and trying to act like a regular fellow."

"Not at all, Nick. It's just that I feel mighty good this year."

"Good for you. I'll give you my Christmas list, and you can go take care of it. Better still, you can write my story for me."

"Hey, I'll do that. Of course, I don't know much about sports." His eyes suddenly danced, and he said, "Did you hear the story about the sportswriter that was given the assignment of writing an obituary?"

"No, but if they gave it to me, I wouldn't do it."

"Well, everybody else was out of town, and this lady died. He tried to get out of it, but his editor insisted. So, he wrote her obituary in the form of a poem. Want to hear the poem?"

"I think I'm about to."

"Here it is:

> Here lie the bones of Nancy Jones;
> For her death held no terrors.
> She lived an old maid; she died an old maid:
> No hits—no runs—no errors."

Nick suddenly laughed. "That's pretty good. I'll remember that."

"Your family doin' good, Nick?"

It was the first time Ben had ever asked about his family, and Nick nodded. "Yeah, they're doing fine."

"Good. Well, got to get to work. Have a glorious Christmas."

Nick stared at Ben as he disappeared inside the building and finally shook his head. "What's got into Ben? He never acted peculiar before."

Ben encountered several of his fellow reporters and greeted them all with a hearty Merry Christmas. He did the same with the clerks and secretaries and stopped by his boss's office. He saw Sal working furiously, his brow furrowed up. Opening the door, he said, "Hey, boss!"

Sal looked up and frowned. "What do you want?"

"Just wanted to say Merry Christmas."

"Never mind that stuff. How's that story coming? I've got to have it pretty soon."

"Going to be the best Christmas story you ever heard."

As Raines turned and went down the hall whistling "Rudolph the Red-Nosed Reindeer," Sal watched him go. "I think he needs a vacation. He's going nutty on me."

• • •

Willie was taken aback as Ben came through the door. His son's face lit up, and he came up and gave Willie a hug. It caught Willie off guard. Ben was not given to gestures of affection like this. "How are you doing, Dad?"

"Fine, Ben. What have you been up to?"

"Oh, the same old stuff. I just came by to talk to you."

"Sit down."

Willie watched, aware that something was bubbling over inside Ben's spirit. He was all he had left in the world, his only relative, and it had grieved him that Ben turned out to be so negative toward the world around him. Now he saw something working in him, and he said, "What's going on?"

"I just wanted to give you a report on Billy Bob. Charlene and I had a great visit with him."

"He's doing good? That's great. I always liked Billy Bob. We keep in touch, you know."

"He told me. I brought a letter for you from him." He took the envelope out and said, "He said to wish you a Merry Christmas."

A fond look came into Willie's eyes. "He was always up to something. I never knew a fellow could scrounge like he would. The rest of the company would be starving to death, and Billy Bob would come in with a rabbit or a chicken, something that he had scrounged. We always shared it no matter how little it was."

"Well, he thinks highly of you. Did you know he won the Congressional Medal of Honor?"

"Oh sure, I knew about that. He never talks about it himself, though."

"No. His wife told me. She's a fine lady. They've got a fine family." He talked about their visit with Billy Bob, and finally his eyes lit up. "I've got something else to tell you, Dad."

"What's that?"

"We had engine trouble coming back. I thought the plane was going down."

"Well, it didn't, did it? You're here."

"No, it didn't, but I thought it was. It shook me up, Dad, and when we finally landed, I couldn't stop thinking about it." Ben's face grew serious, and he sat very still on the chair across from his father. "I know you haven't been happy with the way I've lived my life. To tell you the truth, I haven't been happy either. But when I thought I was going to die, it changed something, Dad. It made me think in a way nothing ever had."

Ben went on to tell how he had been so shaken that he could hardly speak, and then he said, "Charlene talked to me about becoming a Christian. I guess it was my time, Dad." His face lit up, and he reached out and squeezed his father's hand. "Because that's what I did. I just called on the Lord, and ever since that time I've been different."

Tears came into Willie's eyes. He was not a man that showed emotion like this much, but he put his hand over Ben's and cleared his throat. "That's . . . that's the best news I ever heard, Ben."

The two men sat there, their hands intertwined, and Benjamin Raines knew that things could never be the same between him and his dad again.

The two talked for awhile, and finally Ben said, "I've got one more flight with Charlene—to Florida to interview Roger Saunders."

"I've been out of touch with Roger. He moves around a lot. Give him my best and wish him Merry Christmas."

"I'll do that, Dad. When I come back, we're going to have the best Christmas you ever thought about." He reached over again and hugged his father, and when he left, Willie Raines moved over to the window. When Ben came out and headed for the parking lot, Willie's eyes followed him. He reached down, got his handkerchief, and wiped his eyes and whispered, "Lord, it's been a long wait, but I thank You for saving my boy!"

Chapter
ELEVEN
༃

Charlene sat facing Willie Raines, watching his face with a glow of pleasure. The two had been playing checkers, and she suddenly laughed aloud. "Do you *ever* lose a game, Willie?"

Willie rubbed his chin and looked up thoughtfully at the ceiling. "Well, it seems to me that I did lose a game back in 1932." He suddenly laughed and said, "Sure. I've lost plenty of them." He studied the young woman across from him and now spoke his thought aloud. "You know I've been wondering how Ben ever managed to talk you into flying him over the whole country. You're a busy woman. I know that."

"It's been fun, Willie," Charlene said. "I've always been interested in the men that served with my dad, and I've meant to get in touch with them, but it was one of those things I just put off."

"Well, you sure made Ben's work a sight easier," Willie said. "Where are you going next?"

"We're going down to Florida to see Roger Saunders."

"Roger Saunders. Hey, that brings back memories! He was different from the rest of us fellows."

Charlene leaned forward, her eyes intent. "Different how, Willie?"

"Well, for one thing, he was smarter than the rest of us. He wasn't too good a shot and not much with anything mechanical, but he was a thinker. You could tell that. When we got the news about the war, he'd tell us what it all meant. Made me a little nervous to be around a man that smart, but he was a good soldier."

The two talked for some time about the members of the squad, and then Willie said, "I can't tell you how good it's made me feel knowing that Ben came to the Lord. Been praying for him all of his life, I guess, and his mom did, too, before she went on."

"He's different, isn't he?"

"I'll tell the world! He looks different, he talks different, and there's a light in his eyes."

"It's made me very happy. I haven't known Ben long, but the Lord gave me a burden for him."

Their conversation was interrupted when Charlene lifted her head. "I hear him coming."

"I can't hear him, but I can hear Mabelene. She thinks everybody's deaf, I guess. Talks like it anyway."

Ben suddenly appeared in the open door with Mabelene right behind him. The two entered, and Ben walked at once over to Willie and gave him a hug. "How you doin', Pop?"

"Doin' fine, Son."

Charlene saw how much the gestures meant to Willie Raines, and she smiled. "Don't I get a hug, too?"

"Have you been good?"

"Not particularly."

"Well then, no hugs until you're good."

Mabelene was watching this with her eyes wide. "What about you? Have you been good?"

Ben suddenly turned to face the nurse. She was a tall woman, broad and strong, and had not completely accepted the idea that Ben was now a believer.

"Mabelene, I've changed so much I'm going to give you a Christmas present."

"Humph! What kind of present you gonna give me?"

Ben had his head turned to one side and winked at Willie and Charlene. "Well, I've been shopping down at Victoria's Secret, and I found—"

"I don't want to hear nothin' about what you found at that place!" Mabelene said, her lips drawn together in a straight line. "That ain't nothin' but a sinful place!"

Willie began to laugh, and Charlene could not keep her smile back. "He's teasing you, Mabelene."

Mabelene glared at Ben and then saw that he was trying to suppress his own smile. "You keep your old Victoria Secrets stuff! You wanna give me a present I'll tell you what to give me."

"All right. You tell me, and I'll give it to you."

"You promise?"

"Sure. What is it?"

"I want you to come to our church for the special Christmas service."

"Why, I'll do that, Mabelene. It'll be a pleasure. Maybe Dr. Delaughter would like to go, too."

"Of course I would. We'll both go."

Mabelene's face grew cheerful. "All right then. I got your promise. I'll be lookin' for you." She turned and left the room, and Ben shook his head. "She's something, isn't she? Are you about ready to go?"

"All ready, Ben."

"You give Roger my best. I wish I could see him. I wish I could see all of them, but you tell him that I think about him a lot."

"I'll tell him, Dad." He went over and rested his hand on Willie's shoulder and squeezed it. "You hold the fort here. We'll be back as soon as we can, and we're gonna have one bodacious Christmas celebration right here in this hospital."

As they walked down the hall, Charlene was quiet. "What's wrong with you?" Ben asked. "Is something the matter?"

"I was just thinking how happy you've made your dad."

Ben did not speak for a time, and when they were outside, he turned his coat collar up against the chilly breeze. "I'm ashamed at the way I treated dad."

"Well, you can make it up to him," Charlene smiled. "That's one good thing. I wish I could make things up to my dad."

"Were you two close?"

"Very close, but I miss him, and I think of things I could have done for him, but I didn't."

The two walked down toward Charlene's car, and when they got in, she said, "It's good flying weather."

"Well, I don't want to go down, but at least I'll be ready if we do."

Charlene laughed. "Don't talk like that. We're gonna have a great flight."

. . .

"That must be it right over there. See? Slip thirteen."

Charlene pointed toward one of the large houseboats that lined the harbor at the docks. They were numbered, and Ben had told her that Roger Saunders's boat was in the thirteenth slot, which was called a slip. The boats moved slightly in the water as a wind over the sea lifted them. The two headed down toward the boat and Ben said, "That must be him."

Charlene saw a man sitting in the front of the boat. His back was to them, and he appeared to be asleep.

Ben looked over and said, "The Logos. That's the name of his boat. What does that mean?"

"It means the *word*. You know, like in John 1, 'In the beginning was the word.' He named his boat after Jesus, really."

"That's neat," Ben smiled with admiration. They moved closer to the dock, and Ben called out, "Mr. Saunders?"

The man snorted, shook his shoulders, and got to his feet hurriedly. He was a small, compact man with deep-set eyes that appeared to be very dark blue. His face was weathered by sun and wind, the look of a sailor. He smiled and walked over to the short gangplank. "Come aboard," he said. "I expect you must be Ben Raines."

"That's right. This is Dr. Charlene Delaughter."

"Doctor, it's good to have you." He shook hands with both of them and stepped aside. "Come aboard. It's kind of cold out here, but it's warm down in the cabin. Could you drink some coffee—cocoa?"

"Anything hot," Ben said. "That would be good."

The three of them went below, and Charlene exclaimed, "Why, this is beautiful!"

It was indeed a beautiful room. The walls were of walnut that glowed with a sheen. The carpet on the floor was as thick as any that Charlene had ever seen. There were couches along two sides and large windows that admitted the sunlight.

"I've never been on a boat like this."

"Only way to live," Roger Saunders said. "You want decaf, regular, cocoa, espresso? I'm gonna put Starbucks out of business."

He made the coffee, and they sat down around the table. Ben said at once, "As I told you on the phone, Mr. Saunders, I'm writing a story about the squad you were in back at Bastogne."

"I know. I've been thinking about it. It wasn't much fun."

"No, it couldn't have been, but I'd like to put something in the story about it. So, if you'll tell me how you remember it, it might help. . . . I'd like to tape it, if you don't mind."

"Been a long time ago." Roger hesitated and said, "How's your dad?"

"Well, he's getting on, but he's bright and cheerful. He's in the VA Hospital, as I told you. I tried to take care of him, but I couldn't, going out to work."

"You're not married?"

"No. Just me and him."

"Well, I'll tell you what I remember about that time." Roger Saunders began to speak, and he had a marvelous way with words. He described that bitter, cold winter and the terrible conditions that the men lived through, and as he spoke, the memories seemed to flow.

Finally he ended and moved a hand across his forehead. "We lost a lot of good men there. Most of our squad didn't make it."

It seemed to have troubled him to talk about the war. Suddenly he proposed, "What do you say we take her out for a bit?"

"I don't know. We don't want to take your time, Mr. Saunders."

"Just Roger will do. I always go out for awhile about this time of day. Then I'll cook you a supper when we come back, if you're not in a hurry."

"No hurry at all, and it'll be interesting to go out in a houseboat."

• • •

The trip was fine, and Ben and Charlene enjoyed it. Roger handled the wheel easily through the open water. The houseboat was not fast but forged steadily along through the gray-green water. When the shore was almost out of sight, Roger looked around at the open space and said, "I try to get out here every day. Florida's getting to be a big tourist trap."

"Everybody wants a bit of the sun and fun, I guess."

"You know, I went to Israel once. I had it in my mind that it'd look like the pictures in my Bible storybook," Roger grinned. "Now there's a big tourist trap! They would take us to a place and say, 'Right here, this was where Lazarus was raised.' How in the world would they know that? There were no historians or photographers standing around to mark the spot."

"I had the same experience," Charlene said. "Most of it was disappointing."

"You know the one place that wasn't disappointing?" Roger asked. "We got in a small boat and went out on the Sea of Galilee. The guide stopped the motor, and we sat there. It was quiet that day, no high waves. The guide said, 'Just like it was when Jesus was here. No tourist traps.'"

"I thought that when I was up in the mountains of Israel. They haven't changed. No souvenir shops there," Charlene said. They talked for awhile about Israel, and for a time they simply cruised along. It was quiet and peaceful, and after a time Roger said, "I've got some fresh red snapper. Caught it myself. Why don't you just steer the boat while I go cook 'em up?"

Ben was alarmed. "Why, I don't know how to drive one of these!"

"Just don't run into anything," Saunders grinned.

"But I'll get us lost."

"Well, I'll get us found. That's what that thing right there is for." He pointed to the instrument panel. "Doc, why don't you come and help me do the cooking."

"All right, I will." The two headed down to the cabin and left Ben alone. He was alarmed, for he knew nothing about seamanship. It gave him a strange feeling to control the boat, and as he did, he thought about how nice it would be to live like Roger Saunders. *If you don't like one place,* he thought, *you just start the engine up and go someplace else.*

Several times he saw boats off in the distance, and from time to time a plane would go over, but the rest was peace and quiet. *I could take a month or two of this*, he thought.

• • •

The dinner was fine—fresh red snapper, grilled and blackened, with hush puppies to go with it and a fresh garden salad.

"I heard about hush puppies and had them in a restaurant in Chicago," Charlene said, "but they were nothing like these. They're delicious."

"I got the recipe from a fellow that came from Orange Beach, Alabama. He ran a charter boat there. He was some cook."

"How do you get fresh garden stuff this time of the year?"

"Oh, it's not like Chicago. We get fresh stuff most of the time around here," Roger said. He drank from his glass of iced tea and said, "Now tell me about the rest of the squad." He sat there and listened and finally, when Ben had numbered them, he turned and looked at Charlene and said, "So your dad's the only one that's not with us anymore."

"That's right. I lost Dad a few years ago, but he had a good life. I miss him though."

"I know you do." Roger hesitated, then said, "I'll tell you about myself. I don't know how much of it needs to go into the story, but I'll let you decide that."

The stereo was playing classical music in a soft, muted tone. Roger's voice was quiet, and he seemed to go back into time as he began to speak.

"Well, I survived the war, but it made a cynic out of me. I saw too many good guys die. I came home and tried to pick up my life. Went back to college but got in with the wrong bunch. Got into drinking and dope—bad stuff. My wife had waited for me all through the war, but she couldn't handle all that. She finally left me."

Ben listened, studying the man's face. His host had a thin and taut face, and his eyes were quick and alert. He remembered his dad had said Roger Saunders was one of the smartest men he ever knew.

"It's an old story. I lost everything through my drinking. Woke up one morning in jail. Funny thing, it was Christmas week. Everybody on the street was buying presents. That didn't mean anything to me. All I was thinking about was my next drink.

"When I got out, I didn't have a place to go. No money." He touched his chin thoughtfully and shook his head. "Finally I decided life wasn't worth living. I decided to commit suicide." He saw their faces change and said, "People do it all the time. What did I have to live for?"

He suddenly smiled and said, "You know what my big

problem was? I couldn't figure out a right way to do myself in. That's the trouble with being an intellectual. You think about things too much. I didn't have a gun and no money to buy one. I didn't know how to get poison or which kind to get. Somehow I couldn't stand the idea of using a knife."

Ben grinned. "Well, obviously, you didn't find the right way."

"No," Roger said. "I decided to jump off the tallest building in town. That was the economical way, you see. Didn't even have to buy a gun or poison. I went there. They were having trouble with the elevator, and I decided to walk up to the top floor. It was twenty stories high. By the time I got there I was pretty well winded, completely out of shape. I found the access to the roof and went out there. It was cold. The wind was whistling. I could see the lights of the city—Christmas lights, that is, everywhere. It looked beautiful, but it didn't mean anything to me. I went up to the edge of the building, to the ledge there, and I got out on it and sat there. It was harder than I thought, but I sat there freezing to death."

He picked up his glass and took a sip of tea. "I thought about something while I was there. I had known a woman once, a very wealthy woman. She decided to kill herself by jumping off a building. She told me about it afterward. She went to the finest hotel in the city. She was in New York. Got an expensive room, opened the window, and climbed up on the sill. Then she looked down and saw that her toenails weren't painted." Roger laughed. "She told me she couldn't stand the idea of people seeing her with her toenails not done nicely. So she came in to go get some nail polish before she jumped, but she never did go through with it."

"Well, I didn't care much about what my toenails looked like. I was just about to go when I heard a voice behind me. It scared me so bad I nearly fell off that blasted building!"

The boat rose slowly and then sank as a wave lifted it. It was odd to Ben being in a room that wouldn't stand still, but he was fascinated with Saunders' story. "What did you do, Roger?"

"Well, the guy came forward. He wore a jacket that had the name of an elevator company. I forget what it is now. He came to work on the elevator, and I just stared at him. Finally, I think, I asked him what he was doing out on Christmas Day. He was an average-looking guy, you know. Workmen look pretty much alike. He told me that he had had a call to come out and look at the elevator."

"Didn't he think it strange you were sitting on the edge of a building twenty stories high in the middle of winter?"

Roger laughed. "I'm sure he did. And you know what I thought of? I thought of that movie, *It's a Wonderful Life*. Remember how Jimmy Stewart's guardian angel caught him just as he was about to jump in and drown himself in the river? I thought about that."

Charlene was watching Roger Saunders carefully. "What did he say?"

"He said his name was Jerzy Wienckyslaw. He told me that he met this woman and fell in love with her. She was a Polish woman. Her name was Katrine Chudzik." He suddenly stopped and said, "I remember those names after all these years. Anyway, he told me that she had led him to Jesus, and then he asked me to come home with him."

"Come home with him? What for?"

"He didn't say, but I was in bad shape. To tell the truth, I needed somebody pretty bad. I went home with him, and they took me in. They dried me out and prayed for me. They loved me, Ben, and I knew it. They weren't phony. I lived with them for a month, and I knew that God was real because I saw Him in them. So one night I asked God to save me and prayed in the name of Jesus, and He did."

"That's a wonderful story, Roger," Charlene said.

"Well, it was a rocky road back, but I had a lot on my side. God gave me a new wife and three children. My wife died a few years ago, but the kids are doing well."

"What'd you do for a living all these years?" Ben asked curiously. "They don't give boats like this away."

"No. The Lord blessed me. I started out to be an engineer, but that didn't work. I've always been interested in writing, so I started writing. Wound up writing fiction."

Ben turned his head. "I read quite a bit, but don't believe I've read any of your books."

"I don't write under my own name. You lose your privacy that way."

"What name do you write under?"

"James Lawrence."

Ben stared speechlessly at Roger Saunders. "You're James Lawrence?"

"No. I'm Roger Saunders. I just use that name to keep a little privacy."

"I've read all your books. They're great," Ben stammered. He could not believe what he was hearing.

"I've read some of them too," Charlene added. "There are so many bad books out on the market, and it's refreshing to read one that's good and believes in good."

"I always want my books to be a blessing to people," Roger said. He smiled and added, "Don't tell anyone who I am or I wouldn't be able to live like I do."

The three sat up until late talking, and finally Ben got up and said, "We've kept you up a lot of hours."

"That's all right, Ben. It's so good to hear about Willie, and I'm glad to hear about you, too." His eyes went to Charlene, and he winked at her. "You take care of this man. Make a good writer out of him."

He turned to Ben, and for what seemed like a long moment he was silent. Finally something changed in his face. "You tell your dad, Ben, that he gave me a chance. If it weren't for him, I'd never have written a single word."

• • •

All the way back to Chicago, Ben and Charlene talked about how strange it was that one of the men Willie had saved was now a famous writer.

"Why, he's won so many prizes for his writing I couldn't name them. He's blessed people all over the world, Charlene."

"I know, and he's such a modest man, too. You can tell he really loves God."

"I can't wait to get back and tell Dad about this." He reached over then and took her free hand. He held it and said, "It's been great, hasn't it, all of it?"

Charlene was intensely aware of the warmth of his grasp. "Yes," she whispered, "it has been great."

The stars overhead glittered with warmth. As the plane made its way through the skies, the two in the plane felt they were enclosed not in an airplane but in God's creation.

Chapter
TWELVE

Christmas came rushing toward Ben at a rapid pace. He worked hard on his story and took Charlene out twice. During the last week before Christmas they had dinner together. Ben talked about his plans to have Christmas dinner with his dad and was pleased when Charlene asked if she could join the party.

"Why, sure you can, but I thought you'd have other plans."

"I can't think of anything I'd rather do or anybody I'd rather be with."

Charlene was wearing a black knit dress with a high collar and sleeves that formed a slight bell at the wrists. It seemed to skim over her body and fell to just below her knees. Her hair was hanging down but was tucked behind her ears, showing off a pair of pearl earrings. Ben suddenly grinned. "I thought doctors always had emergencies on Christmas."

"That's possible, but I'm not going to plan for it."

The two went for a drive out by the lake. A snow had fallen the night before, and the pristine beauty of the moonlight on the water caught both of them. He parked the car and turned to her. "You know, I've never looked forward to Christmas like I am to this one."

"Not even when you were young?"

"Not even then."

They sat there talking, running the engine to keep the car warm, and finally he said, "I want to give you something nice for Christmas. What do you want?"

"Dedicate your first book to me."

Ben smiled, then reached over and took her hand. "I was going to do that anyway."

"What do you want for Christmas?" Charlene asked.

Ben was quiet for such a long time that Charlene wondered about it. "Was that too hard for you, Ben?"

"No. I know exactly what I want. I want us to be together." He lifted his eyes, and in the silvery moonlight he saw that her lips were parted slightly and she was watching him carefully. "You mean to be friends?" she asked.

"I think we're already that, but I want more than that. I want you to come to think of me as a man you might marry." Ben saw that her eyes widened, and he said quickly, "I know it's too soon for that, but I'm warning you my worst flaw is stubbornness. I'd like for us to grow old together, Charlene. False teeth, Metamucil, forgetting where we put our glasses. All that kind of stuff."

"That's a wonderful proposal. I'll bet no man in the world ever put Metamucil in his proposal to a woman."

"What do you think of it?" Ben lifted her hand, kissed it, and said, "I know—let's go steady!"

Charlene suddenly laughed. "I haven't heard that expression in years. You mean like in high school?"

"Sure."

"The last time I went steady was when I was sixteen years old. I agreed to go steady with Norm Obermeyer."

"Good old Norm."

"Well, I didn't like him much, but it was my first offer."

Ben stroked her hand. "How long did it last?"

"I think it was three weeks. Maybe it was only two. I can't remember. Betty Hodges was one of the cheerleaders. She took him away from me."

"Norm was kind of a dork. Betty Hodges didn't have anything."

"You didn't even know her."

"No, but I know you. What about it?" he said. "You want to go steady?"

"I think so."

Ben expelled his breath. "I thought you'd say no."

"That's what it is, Ben. Just going steady. Seeing each other. Getting married is too big a thing to be wrong about."

"I know. I'll be on trial. You'll begin to check all my habits to see if I qualify."

"And you can check all of mine."

Ben moved closer and put his arms around her. "Don't you think," he whispered, "that two people who have decided to go steady should make some kind of gesture? You know, just so they know where they are?"

Charlene's lips curved upward at the corners in a smile. "You mean like give each other name bracelets?"

"No. I mean like this." He was watching her carefully and saw her eyes widen as he drew her close. Her eyes were soft gray, and the light danced in them. He saw her lips lengthen and then he kissed her, his mouth bearing down hard and heavy on hers. When he lifted his lips, she asked him suddenly, "What's the woman like, Ben, the woman you want?"

Ben sat very still, aware of the warmth and the firmness of her as he held her, and Charlene knew that her question had reached into the deepest place of his makeup. She knew suddenly that the picture of a woman was in him, colored and rounded, and yet she knew that he had no words that could describe what he felt.

"Like you," he said simply. "I didn't know there was a woman like you."

Charlene felt warm and content and fulfilled. "There's been an emptiness in me, Ben. I've been lonely and afraid to face the future alone, but now I know that I don't have to."

They sat there silently for a time, and suddenly she turned toward him. "I'm going to give your dad a gift."

"Well, he's a little bit hard to buy for."

"I know, but he'll like this one." She squeezed his hand between both of hers and said, "Let me tell you about it. . . ."

Chapter
THIRTEEN
乷

M abelene stepped back and turned her head to one side. "My, don't you look handsome!"

Willie had donned new clothes that Ben had brought to him for the Christmas party. He had gotten a haircut and had shaved carefully. Mabelene had come in to check him over, and now she said, "You know what'll make you look really good?"

"What's that, Mabelene?"

"Cornrows. Now they'd make you look really spiffy."

Willie laughed. "I don't think I've got what it takes for cornrows, Mabelene."

"No, I guess not. That boy of yours," she said suddenly, "he serious about that lady doctor?"

"He's serious as income tax."

"I asked around about her from doctors I know. They say she's really OK."

"Why, I'm glad that you approve."

"You know," Mabelene said, "it don't hurt to have a doctor around at times."

"You mean when you're sick?"

"No," Mabelene smiled broadly, "Dr. Delaughter, she used her influence here in the hospital to get her own way. You're gonna get to use the board room for a private Christmas dinner. Ain't that a caution? Nobody has ever got to use the board room for nothin' like that."

Mabelene had just turned to go when Ben and Charlene entered the room. "Hello, Mabelene," Ben said. "Here's your present." He handed her a package, and she glanced at him suspiciously. "It didn't come from that old Victoria Secrets, did it?"

"No, it came from the Bible book store. I think you'll like it."

"I'll put it under the tree, and remember you promised to go to our Christmas program at the church. It's tomorrow night."

"I'll be there."

"And so will I," Charlene said. She handed Mabelene a small, gaily-wrapped package. "Merry Christmas."

"Why shoot, Doctor, I didn't get you nothin'."

"You can get me something next year."

Ben said, "I think the meal's all ready."

"I told Sergeant Raines here about you gettin' the private board room. I don't know how you arranged that. They didn't let nobody else do it."

"Rank has its privileges," Charlene smiled. "You come on down later, Mabelene, and sample some of the meal we put together."

"I'll maybe do that."

Ben got behind Willie's wheelchair and said, "All right, Pop, time for a great Christmas dinner."

Ben wheeled Willie down the corridor. They took the elevator and went to the third floor where the board room was. Charlene opened the door, and when they went in, Willie gasped, "Well, look at this!"

The board room had been converted into a miniature banquet room. The long table was covered with a tablecloth, white with bells and ivy pattern. The table was all set, and over to the right two men stood beside a serving table designed to keep food hot. A stereo was playing Christmas music quietly, and Willie was overwhelmed. "This is really something!" he said.

"Oh, you ain't seen nothing yet, Dad. My doctor friend is quite a lady. She has a gift for you."

Willie glanced over at the artificial tree that had packages stacked up under it. "I hope it ain't socks. I hate socks for Christmas presents."

"Oh, it's better than socks. Too big to put under your tree. Go ahead, Charlene."

Charlene came over and bent over Willie. She took his hands and said, "I wanted to make this a Christmas that you'd never forget. You gave my dad the best Christmas present he could have had—his life. And I had him for a long time. That was your present to me, Willie. But I thought, *What would I get a man who had done such a thing for me?*"

"Not neckties either. I don't like neckties."

"No neckties. Are you ready?"

"Guess so."

Willie expected Charlene to go over and pick a gift out

from under the tree, but instead she walked over to a door to her left and opened it. She stepped back, and Willie's eyes opened wide when he saw who came through it.

"Willie, you old son of a gun!"

"Chief!" Willie said. He knew the man instantly even though he had not seen him for years. "Chief Shoulders!"

"It's me all right, Sarge." Shoulders came over, his black eyes snapping. He leaned over and took Willie's hand. Then he reached back and put his arm around him and held him close. When he released Willie and stepped back, he said, "Look at me. I'm crying just like I was a silly woman."

Indeed, Lonnie Shoulders did have tears in his eyes. "I should have done this a long time ago, Willie." He wiped his eyes and said, "It's going to be hard. I've never quite forgiven you for putting me on all that latrine duty."

Willie was overjoyed and held onto Chief's hand. "I got you a present," Chief said. "You may not like it, but it's one of a kind. You'll never get another present like this."

"You're all the present I need, Chief. I can't tell you how glad I am to see you."

Chief turned and walked over toward the door. "Here it is." He opened the door, the same door he had come through, and suddenly a man came through dressed in the uniform of the 101st Airborne. The uniform was too big now, for Pete Maxwell had shrunk. His cheeks were drawn, but he was grinning broadly. "Sarge, I'm glad to see you."

"Pete!" Willie took one of Pete's hands in both of his and clung to it. "I can't believe it. I just can't believe it!"

"Wait until after we get through puttin' this food away. I'm gonna do my Clark Gable imitation for you, and maybe I'll do some card tricks, too."

Willie could not speak he was so overcome. He looked at Charlene and said, "You couldn't have gotten me a present I like any better. Two presents, that is."

"No, three," she said and walked toward the door. She spoke and Roger Saunders walked through. He was wearing gray slacks and a blue sweater, and he looked handsome with his silver hair and blue eyes. "Willie, it's been too long." He came over and shook Willie's hand. "I've thought about you for fifty years, believe it or not. We should have kept up with each other better."

"Roger, how have you been?"

"I've been fine."

Willie clung to Roger's hand and said, "It's not like that Christmas at Bastogne, is it?"

"Nothing was like that."

"One more present, Dad," Ben said. He called out, "Come in, whoever you are."

Billy Bob Watkins strolled in—raw-boned, lanky, his tow hair a little thinner than the last time Willie remembered, but really still the same.

"Ain't this a kick in the head?" he said, dancing across the room. He reached over and tapped Willie on the shoulder with his big fist, then he said, "You and me, we got lots of talkin' to do."

Willie sat there looking around at the four men who gathered around him in a semi-circle. He looked at Charlene and said, "I wish Charlie was here."

"He'd be here if he could."

Willie looked around and said, "A man couldn't have a better Christmas."

"Now, let's eat this food," Charlene said, "and then you five have some catching up to do."

• • •

The meal had been outstanding. Only Billy Bob Watkins had anything negative to say. "This dressin' ain't got cornbread in it." He shook his head sadly. "There wasn't never no good dressin' made north of St. Louis."

After the meal was over each man made his little speech and told Willie how much they owed to him. Each of them had filled a photograph album, all of them the same. Charlene had sent the albums to them and requested this. Each contained pictures of their families and a history of their lives. Willie sat glowing with happiness.

Finally, after the members of the squad had done their duty and spoken, Ben said, "It's your turn, Dad."

Willie Raines looked around the room. He felt a lump in his throat and had to clear it before he could say, "I keep thinking about that line in that poem Charlie told me about. 'We few, we happy few, we band of brothers.'" Willie's hands were not steady as he touched his chin and gazed around the room. "That's what we were—a band of brothers."

"Still are," Chief Shoulders said. "Always will be."

"That's right," Roger Saunders said. "All of us that went through that time are brothers."

"You dadgum betcha," Billy Bob Watkins nodded, "and ain't nothin' gonna change it."

"I got one more present for you, Dad." Ben held up a sheaf of papers and said, "This is my present to you. It's the story. . . . I was assigned to write about Christmas," he said to the men who were watching. "The title is 'Willie Raines and the Angel of Bastogne.' I'd like to read it for you. It starts out, 'I spent most of my life not believing in much, but now I believe in many things. This Christmas I believe in God, and I believe in sacrifice, for I have seen it in my father. I believe that every man and every woman has a chance to give a gift that never dies, as my dad did." He looked up and winked at his father. "And I believe in the Angel of Bastogne!"

THE END